'Til Death

Nadine Zawacki

'Til Death

Copyright 2014 by Nadine Zawacki

ISBN 978-1-978852-00-4

Author: You may contact the author via her blog site:
http://justbeingme1.blogspot.com

This work of fiction describes dysfunctional and abusive relationships. The author encourages anyone in these circumstances to seek help from a trained mental health counselor or a local minister.

Publisher: Wood Island Prints; 670 Trans-Canada Highway, RR 1 Belle River, PE C0A 1B0; (902) 962-3335. Email and web: *schultz@pei.sympatico.ca   www.woodislandsprints.com/*

Printer: Lightning Source Inc. (US); 1246 Heil Quaker Blvd, La Vergne, TN 37086; USA; (615) 213-5815. Email and web: *inquiry@lightningsource.com   www.lightningsource.com*

Scripture taken from *The Message.* Copyright @1993, 1994, 1995, 1996, 2000, 2001, 2002. Used by permission of NavPress Publishing Group.

Cover layout by Thomas Schultz.

Additional copies of Nadine's books may also be ordered at *www.amazon.com*

Then God ordered me,
"Start all over:
Love your wife again,
your wife who's in bed
with her latest boyfriend,
your cheating wife.
Love her the way I, God,
love the Israelite people...."

Hosea 3:1a The Message

Prologue

Restlessness overwhelmed Henry as he lay in bed. He counted sheep, an activity that proved futile, so he decided to get up so he wouldn't disturb his wife. They'd been married nearly fifty years, and Henry cherished every one of them. He was a blessed man to share his life with Ida, his first and only love. He watched her from the foot of the bed for what seemed to be an eternity but was just mere moments. His thoughts drifted back to their wedding day. She was the most beautiful woman he had ever laid his eyes on. Her once auburn hair was as long as it had been on the day they wed. She kept it normally in a tight bun, but at night it framed the soft features of her face. Her blue eyes had the ability to see right through him often to his amusement. Ida dedicated her whole life to their children, kept a comfortable home, and supported him in everything he did. She loved him in spite of his idiosyncrasies; for this he was indebted. Henry was astounded by all the thoughts that flooded his mind with just a passing glimpse of the woman who encompassed his world.

When he looked around the small cabin, it seemed dark except for the night-lights strategically placed around the room. Outside, the wind sounded like someone was singing a sad love song. The sounds of nature usually comforted him, whether it was rain or wind, but not tonight.

Henry headed for the bedroom door when suddenly he sensed a presence behind the door. He opened it slowly but didn't see anything. His heartbeat accelerated for he knew that Samuel was in the room. He took a deep breath and turned around. In the middle of the room stood Samuel with his piercing green eyes that Henry couldn't look directly into. The light that surrounded Samuel seemed brighter tonight than usual, as if the sun had risen in his room.

"Trouble sleeping, Henry?" Samuel spoke as if they were having a conversation over tea.

Henry hesitated before uttering, "Yes… a little bit."

"There's another assignment for you. Are you willing?"

Samuel always asked him if he was willing. It was odd to Henry who never thought of his assignments as choices per se. *No* was never a consideration in his mind. There wasn't anything he wouldn't do for God. "Yes, I'm willing. Who would the Lord have me pray for?"

"There's a man named Sal. He's faithful to the Lord, but he doesn't have an intimate knowledge of Him yet. His wife is a troubled soul who repeatedly breaks his heart. There's a small child that will be caught in the middle."

"Oh my, that's dreadful. What would my Lord have me do?"

"He would have you go to New York where Sal lives and observe him from a distance. I will come to you when it's time to intervene. Prepare to be there a while."

"Can Ida come with me since it's a longer trip?"

"Yes. Leave as soon as possible; there is no time to lose. You know who you can stay with."

With that, Samuel disappeared and the room resumed its original state. Henry rarely ventured out of the comfort of his home to meet his assignments. It was three o'clock in the morning when he returned to bed, and he needed to rest. No need to wake Ida now; he'd explain everything to her in the morning.

Chapter 1

Sal Martinelli sat in the pew for some time after the service was over. Fast asleep, Joey's head laid comfortably on his lap. Sal didn't want to disturb him. He looked so content. Joey was the best thing in his world. He stroked his head lightly, pushed aside his dark brown curly hair from his face. Just like his mother's, Joey's hazel eyes sparkled when he smiled. Sal couldn't believe how quickly he's grown. He'll turn five soon, just in time for kindergarten. *Time moved quicker when you have a kid rather than when you were one.* He gently lifted Joey's head and placed him down on the pew. Sal straightened his pants as he got up more out of habit rather than necessity, just like his father before him. His father came to mind whenever he imitated his behavior. It broke Sal's heart his dad never met his namesake. He scooped Joey up into his arms. With Joey snuggled safely against him, he headed toward the door. There was nothing better than when Joey's head rested on his shoulder. He could feel him breathe against his chest. *It's funny how he could sleep through anything without waking up. The church was now empty except for Father Robert.*

"It's always a pleasure to see you, Salvatore," Father Robert said as he tapped Sal gently on his shoulder.

"You too, Father," Sal whispered.

"Maybe next time your lovely wife could join you and Joseph? It's been too long since I've seen her. Would you send her my regards?"

"Certainly, Father... no problem." *You would think that after all of this time, he'd realize that Vickie was not coming back to church.* "It was a good service. I really enjoyed your homily today on Hosea."

"Thank you. I'll be saying a special prayer for you, son," Father Robert replied.

Nadine Zawacki

"I should get the little guy home," Sal said to end the conversation. He didn't need any *special* prayer. He was good. Vickie was doing better and had been clean for the last six months. Sal hated backhanded conversations. He probably meant well, so he shrugged his shoulders. When he placed Joey in the car, his cell phone rang. He knew who it was before he looked at it and braced himself for the storm named Victoria that was about to hit.

"Hello," he answered after he strapped Joey.

"Where in the hell are you?" he could hear the icicles fall from her lips.

"I'm on my way home."

"I told you a million times, I don't like you taking my kid to *that* place. You snuck out today before I got up. That's not cool, Sally."

He hated it when she called him that and she knew it. "I didn't sneak off with *your* kid. He's half mine and I took my half to church. I can't help it if your half followed."

"Cute, Sally. It should be a crime to put all that God stuff in a little kid's head. He's impressionable."

Sal knew arguing with her would be futile. "I'm on my way home now. Do you need anything?"

"Just the kid!" She hung up the phone.

He wasn't looking forward to going home. When Vickie got mad, she clamped down like a lion on the throat of an antelope. He loved her with his whole heart, but that never seemed to be enough. Lately, he struggled to like her, much less love her. Maybe he's just tired from the long journey they've traveled.

Vickie opened the window and stepped onto the fire escape. She lit her cigarette and savored the first drag. The first one was always her favorite. It comforted her as she inhaled, then exhaled. It wasn't as good as pot but would do in a clinch. *How could he take*

her child to that smelly old church? What had God done for her or him for that matter? I wish he could just loosen up. Why couldn't he be more like Phil? When it came to Sal, once a boy scout always a boy scout. She looked down the street and watched as neighborhood children played stickball. She liked living in Midwood. The neighborhood had both houses and small apartment buildings. Sal wanted to save up for a house one day, but enjoyed the convenience apartment living afforded them. No maintenance was needed—no lawns that needed to be mowed or appliances that needed to be fixed. Granted Brooklyn wasn't known for its massive lawns but the people of Midwood kept what they had well manicured. It was quiet considering the amount of kids that lived on her block. They looked carefree as they laughed and ran around makeshift bases. Funny how manhole covers were always home base. *It's nice to be a kid—no worries, no one to please but yourself.*

The apartment started to close in on her again. Being married felt like living in an amusement park without any money for the rides. She knew Sal loved her, yet it wasn't enough to make her happy. He was a nice guy, maybe *too* nice. She loved him in her own way, but was not sure she was in love with him. If she was honest with herself, he bored her to tears. It didn't matter how many times she screwed up in the past, he was there to pick up the pieces and take her back. *Why would he do that?* She took her last drag and flicked the cigarette. She watched as Sal parallel parked across the street. He looked up, waved and smiled. She hated it when he smiled like that. It was hard to stay mad at him when he had that goofy smile on his face. It charmed her in a weird way.

She went back through the window into the apartment. *Maybe it would just be easier to go away somewhere, anywhere.* Before she knew it, the front door to the apartment opened.

"Mommy, we're home!" Joey said as he ran towards her.

"How's my little man doing?"

"I fell asleep in church," he said proudly.

Vickie smiled at him. *Who could blame you?* "Well I'm sure it was okay. Why don't you go play in your room? I need to have grown up talk with Daddy."

"Is Daddy in trouble?"

"No Buddy," she chuckled. Joey hugged her leg and skipped away towards his room.

Vickie gave Sal a dirty look. She wasn't happy with him. He walked over to her and attempted to give her a hug, but she jerked her body away.

"So... I guess Daddy *is* in trouble."

"That's not funny Sal. You can't take my son to that... that place without asking me first. You know how I feel about it."

"Honey, it's only church. Joey likes going there. He likes the music, and I always take him to breakfast at McDonald's before-hand. I think that's his favorite part." Sal smiled at her again. He placed his hand on the back of her neck and stroked it lightly. "I'm not trying to do things that make you mad, it's just... this means so much to me. It's something we both enjoy." Sal's eyes twinkled as he placed his other hand around her waist. Her resistance was futile. It appeared to Vickie that he would not be deterred by her anger. He looked lovingly into her hazel eyes. "I love you, even when you're upset with me." When he was this close to her, he was hard to resist. His scent caused her mind to drift. It drew her to him. Whether she loved him the way a wife should, didn't interfere with her desire for him physically. His touch was warm. "You know you can't stay mad at me for long. I'm too adorable," he smiled.

She sighed, tilted her head to the side. "You're right. I guess there's no harm done," she moved her face closer to his.

She knew he smelled the cigarette smoke on her breath by his hesitation as she approached him. He hated the fact that she smoked. *He'll have to learn to live with disappointment.* She kissed him passionately. "What's that for?" he asked.

"Are you complaining?"

"No... it just surprised me."

Joey came running into the room. "Mommy... Daddy... look what I made!" he said proudly as he held up a picture he just drawn.

"That's great Buddy, I love it."

"It's a beautiful picture little man," Vickie said.

"It's not beautiful Mommy. I'm a boy... it's handsome."

Vickie looked at Sal, they both tried not to chuckle at his comment. The things that came out of his mouth never ceased to amaze them.

It was moments like these that made life seem normal. "Well Buddy, let's find a placeof honor on the fridge to hang that handsome picture."

"Okay, Daddy," Joey said with excitement.

Vickie felt guilty for wanting to leave. *Who are you kidding; you've never had it so good.* She watched Sal as he placed magnets on Joey's picture to keep it in place.

"Daddy, will you play a game with me?"

"Sure Buddy, whatever you want. Go set it up and I'll be there in a minute." Joey skipped out of the room.

Vickie watched as Sal approached her like he was about to steal a cookie from a jar. He stroked her cheek lightly with the back of his hand and outlined her lips with his finger. "We're good."

"We're good. " He patted her lovingly on her behind. She shook her head. "You know I hate it when you do that."

"You love it," he replied with that goofy grin again.

Vickie smiled as she watched Sal leave. On one hand, she loved her family, and on the other her old life felt like a comfortable pair of old shoes that she didn't care had holes in it. The thrill she felt from her next fix was hard to resist. The escape was euphoric. Her cell phone interrupted her thoughts. It buzzed on the counter. She picked it up and recognized the number. She thought about answering it, but the sound of Joey's squeal from the next room jolted her. The buzzing stopped. She placed the phone back on the counter and walked into the other room.

She witnessed Sal on all fours as Joey rode on his back. She couldn't help but smile, yet the tug she was feeling for her old life wouldn't go away. Six months was the longest stretch she had had without a fix. She pushed the urge aside as she entered into the horseplay with her family.

Chapter 2

Sal knelt by Joey's racecar bed. When they purchased it for his birthday last year, Joey pretended he was a driver in the Indy 500. Like his father before him, NASCAR was one Sal's favorite pastimes. The tradition continued with Joey. Sal gently kissed him on the forehead before he left. He didn't want to wake Vickie before he left, for it's the only time she looked peaceful. He loved to watch her sleep. Her beauty wasn't the only thing that attracted him. Her vulnerability made him feel needed. *Would he have married her even if she weren't pregnant?* Something about her captured his heart. Inventory was an eternal taskmaster, so he needed to get to the store. He grabbed his keys from the hook on the wall next to the door and headed out. He preferred to walk down the stairs instead of taking the elevator. That thing was old, made too much noise and shook as it went up and down. When he reached the front door, he heard a familiar voice call out to him.

"You hoo, Mr. Martinelli!"

He turned around and saw a big smile on Marie Delfeno's face. "Good morning, Mrs. Delfeno. You're up early this morning."

"Why yes," she smiled shyly. "I came out to get my paper... How are you all doing?"

Ah, a loaded question. Translated—how's Vickie and is she still clean? He couldn't fault her with that thought. Mr. & Mrs. Delfeno weren't only good landlords, but also friends. They've helped out with Joey more times than he could count. "We're doing great! How are your knees coming along since the operation?"

She chuckled softly, "Oh, you're such a sweet young man. I've always said to Al how lucky we are to have such a considerate young man living in our building. I'm doing much better. I really like physical therapy. My therapist is a nice young man with great hands. He reminds me of you, not the hands part..." She blushed.

"But he's so kind and gentle... anyway, he reminds me of you."

"Thanks... um... look at the time, I'm running late this morning. Will you give Mr. Delfeno my best?"

"Of course dear. I'm going to bake some chocolate chip cookies today, I'll bring some by for Joey."

"He'll be thrilled. He absolutely loves your homemade cookies."

As he headed for the car, he turned around and looked up at his apartment window. He felt uneasy about leaving today. *Maybe I should just... no, I needed to do inventory and place an order.* He decided to go to work and come home as quick as he could. Margaret could handle things by herself after that. It's not as if there were ever a candy emergency that needed his attention. He wished he could shake the uneasiness he felt. It was probably nothing, probably just his overactive imagination at work.

As she lay on the bed, Vickie stared at the ceiling. She wished being married to Sal was all the satisfaction she needed in life, but it wasn't. He was a good man who loved her but she missed her freedom. She loved her son, but being a wife and mother was tedious and left her unfulfilled. *I feel like a hamster on a wheel, forever moving... never getting anywhere.* Her cell phone rang. She picked it up and saw that it was Phil calling *again*. She paused for a second; thought about Sal's reaction, but decided to answer it anyway. "What do you want?"

"Hey, baby doll. What's with the icy tone?"

"Look Phil, I told you before I can't talk to you."

"Yeah, then why did you answer the phone? I think it's because you miss me."

"What do you want Phil?" she asked sharply, as if she didn't know. The games she played with Phil were to ease her guilty conscience. It somehow justified her actions in her mind if she put up a fight.

"You know what I want. I want you to come out and play." Vickie didn't respond. "It's been too long baby. I miss hangin' with you. I just want to come by... see your pretty face... say hello. Is that so bad?"

"I don't think my husband would like me *hangin'* with you."

"You husband doesn't like a lot of things. Maybe that's why you answered the phone."

"I'm hanging up."

"Wait... wait... don't... aren't we adults? Can't we be friends? There's no crime in talking. Last time I checked talking with a married woman wasn't a sin."

Vickie thought about it for a moment. The sound of his voice comforted her in a peculiar way. Sal would probably be at the store for a while, so she relented. "Okay... but you can't stay long."

"I can't wait to see ya, baby."

Sal's candy store was located on Quentin Road and 35th Street. It was a great location and close to his home. His mother had named it when the store belonged to his father. Sugar Buddies was a simple name that everyone knew, so he saw no need to change it. When Sal pulled up to the candy store, the neon open sign in the window was on. It meant Margaret would be behind the counter, as usual. He was grateful for her diligence. He sat in his car for a moment, wondered why he couldn't shake the feeling that something was wrong. He grabbed his cell phone and was about to call home, when he was startled by a knock on the driver's side window. The last person he expected to see was Rose. He got out of the car. "Rose! What a pleasant surprise. It's been ages since I've seen you." He reached out to hug her, but decided to hold back instead.

"Yeah, it has been." Awkward silence followed. The last time he had seen Rose was the day he met Vickie. It was as if six years had not passed. Her auburn hair cascaded down to her mid back, straight and shinny. Her crystal blue eyes sparkled as they did when they first met. She looked stunning in her fitted blue jeans and red high heels. Rose always overcompensated for her five-foot frame with high heels. He was amazed that she could walk in them. "How have you been?" he asked.

"I've been good. You?"

"Good." Sal had a hard time collecting his thoughts. The sight of her took him right back to when they first met at college orientation. "It's been a long time."

"Yeah," she nodded. "So... how's your... I want to say, son, right?"

"He's amazing. He'll be starting school soon."

"That's good. You look great." Her embarrassment made him smile.

"Thanks. You look like you always did, beautiful." She bit her lower lip as she blushed. He used to love it when she did that. "I heard you got married and moved out of state."

"Yeah... um... my husband died last year in a car accident. That's why I moved back home. It was too hard staying in Washington without him," she said longingly.

The sadness in her eyes moved Sal. He hadn't known about the accident, or that he died. "I'm so sorry to hear that."

The mood had changed as awkwardness draped over them *again*. Rose broke the silence. "It was nice to run into you. Maybe we could have coffee some time and catch up." He nodded his head and smiled.

As Rose walked away he wondered why he broke it off. Oh yeah, Vickie. He wanted to patch up their relationship, but Vickie got pregnant. *Being married to her really turned out well, didn't it? If only he went after Rose that day... it didn't matter now.* He headed inside. Margaret was behind the counter. She looked up when she heard the side door open. "Morning."

"Good morning, Margaret." Margaret was an older woman of

Irish decent, who lost her husband five years ago. She had worked for Sal since. Gray hair and deep wrinkles added a sense of wisdom to her persona. She didn't have any children of her own, but was motherly and protective toward Sal.

"What's wrong?"

"What? Nothing's wrong." Sal tried to sound sincere.

"Well, Salvatore you don't look right. You look like a man with a burden on his heart," she said matter-of-factly.

He never understood how she did that. It was like she could read his mind. "I'm fine. After I do inventory I'm going home for a little while."

"You're the boss. You needn't justify your actions to the likes of me. But if you ask me, you don't look quite right."

"Truly, I'm fine."

She looked at him over her glasses. "As you wish."

He walked into the back room where his small office was located. The room barely had enough space for his desk, much less anything else, but it suited him. He sat down to gather his thoughts. He ran his hands through his hair and controlled the urge to scream. Something was not right with Vickie—he felt it. If life wasn't complicated enough, Rose was back in town. He couldn't believe the old feelings that stirred within him. *What's wrong with you?* He grabbed his clipboard and headed for the storage room to check inventory.

Vickie watched Joey color in his book at the kitchen table. The knock on the door startled her. "You stay put, Joey."

He looked up at her, shrugged his shoulders and said, "Okay, Mommy." He went back to his crayons.

She wiped the sweat from her brow as she approached the front door. She looked in the wall mirror next to the door and noticed a smudge on her face. She quickly dabbed it off and opened the door.

"Good morning, dear. I hope I'm not interrupting." Mrs. Delfeno wasn't whom she expected.

"Not at all. Joey's inside coloring in his book."

"I baked cookies this morning and thought Joey would enjoy some."

"How sweet of you." Vickie noticed Phil coming up the stairs. He had the good sense to back off when he saw she wasn't alone. "Mrs. Delfeno would you like Joey to come down for a visit?" *Quick thinking Vick.*

"I would be delighted," she nearly squealed with excitement.

"Joooooey, come here!"

Joey came running to the front door. He saw the plate of cookies in Mrs. Delfeno's hands. "Mrs. D. is that for me?"

Mrs. Delfeno bent over and handed Joey the plate. "Why don't you give this to your Mom for later."

"Later?"

"Well, I thought you could come down and have some cookies at my house. I just bought a new book that I would love to read to you."

"Yeah! Let's go." Vickie grabbed the plate of cookies from Joey. He hugged her leg and grabbed Mrs. Delfeno's hand.

"You be a good boy now, Joey."

"Okie dokie, Mommy."

"What time would you like me to bring Joey back up?"

"If you don't mind, I'm going to take this opportunity to take a nice nap. I feel a migraine coming on. Would you mind if I came down for Joey when I get up?" *What a tangled web.*

"Of course that's fine. He's welcome to stay as long as you need dear."

Vickie watched Joey skip towards the elevator. She glanced over to the stairs, but didn't see Phil. The elevator door closed. She wondered if Phil left. At that moment, he came back up the steps. He looked at Vickie in a way that made her feel as if she was a piece of rare steak being dangled in front of a hungry lion.

"Hey baby, you're looking good," Phil said as he licked his lips.

"Get in here before someone sees you." She grabbed him by the arm, as she pulled him into the apartment.

His eyes scanned her up and down. As he looked fiercely into her eyes, he said, "You look delicious."

"Stop it! If you came here just to be a pig you can go home."

"Oh baby, such harsh words. We haven't seen each other in a very long time." He walked up to her as he extended his arms. "What... no hug?"

"Seriously, Phil, why are you here?"

"Better question is why did you let me come? You've dodged my calls for months." Phil walked over to the couch and made himself comfortable. He pats the cushion next to him. "Come... sit. I have something for you."

Vickie didn't move. "I've been clean for the last six months, Phil. I don't want anything you have." Even Vickie wasn't convinced of her resolve.

Phil pulled out a little plastic bag. The white powder illuminated in his hand. She took a deep breath. Her glaze fixated on his every action. She watched as he placed a small mirror slowly on the coffee table and proceeded to make those familiar lines. She felt her heart race with excitement. Mesmerized, she inched her way to the couch and sat. At that moment she realized she still had the plate of cookies in her hand. She placed the plate next to the mirror. *I have better control now. A little can't hurt.*

Sal sat at his desk with his feet up. "Look Bryan, I need sugar dots... hey, if you can't supply them then I'll find someone who will... I'm sorry you feel that way... fine!" He placed his feet down and hung up the phone. He hadn't noticed Margaret in the doorway to his small office.

"Anything I can do?"

"No!" He realized the tone he used was harsh. "I'm sorry. I was just talking to Bryan and he wants to raise the rates again on sugar dots and to top it off the shipment will be late. Seriously! It's sugar dots."

"Needn't get yourself in a tizzy. There are plenty of other suppliers out there. Besides, sugar dots are overrated."

Sal chuckled at her attempted humor. "You're probably right, but I've known Bryan for a long time. I'll just call him in a minute and apologize."

"Do you want to talk about it?"

"About sugar dots?"

Margaret shook her head. "Your mood has nothing to do with Bryan or his sugar dots. We both know that."

He didn't want to talk about what the core problem was with anyone. His life had been the subject of too many conversations. "Thanks for asking, but I'm good. I'll probably go home early today."

"Oh."

"What do you mean by 'oh'?"

"You're a good man, but we both know the Mrs. will be the death of ya."

Margaret had a knack of hitting the nail on the head. Sal wasn't ready to admit defeat. "She's just lost, Margaret."
"Have you considered that maybe she wants to stay that way?"

He's had this conversation before. There wasn't a need to continue. "Don't worry so much Margaret. I'm fine... I promise."

"Okay, if you say so. Do you want me to call Bryan and smooth things over? You know I think he's taken a shine to me." She raised her brow.

Sal snickered, "I'm sure he has, but I better do it. I'll go home after I'm done."

Nadine Zawacki

Chapter 3

"Oh Henry, why do we have to go to New York City?"

"Ida honey, don't fret. I've told you…" He caressed her shoulders as he continued, "we're going to be staying with a nice family. There's an adorable little boy who's about three and a beautiful little baby girl. They're expecting us." He continued his massage of her shoulders because it was the only thing that calmed her down when she became nervous.

Ida relented easier than expected. "Henry, you know exactly what to say to me. I love little children and who could resist a little baby girl. Are you sure it's okay that I come along?"

"Of course, Ida. I've called ahead. They're excited to meet you." He looked at her affectionately when he said, "Sweetheart, don't worry. The flight will be fine. I'll be with you the whole time." He gave her a hand a little squeeze. "Right by your side as always."

She took a deep breath. "You're a good man, Henry James. Let me finish packing while you go pray. See if the Lord will tell you anymore about our trip."

She was so in tuned with his needs. It was one of the many reasons he loved her. He walked outside his little cabin. The massive rainfall the night before left puddles in his yard. He loved the smell of fresh rain that hung in the air for it reminded him of his mother. She loved walks in the rain and he loved when she took him along. They would discuss anything that was on his heart. She would say the rain was God's way of giving the earth a bath. Henry's thoughts drifted back to the present. Large oak trees surrounded his cabin like soldiers that protected the perimeter of his home. At least he liked to pretend they were. It was peaceful to be out in the middle of nowhere. He closed his eyes and suddenly he was on a mountaintop. He saw with his mind's eye two large rocks. A large eagle was perched on top of the rock on the right. Henry knelt down on the wet ground. He trembled with fear. The mountaintop swiftly filled with light. Henry didn't dare open his eyes.

He heard a voice say, "There is much pain ahead for your young charge. The temptation to interfere will be great. A work needs to be done in his heart. Don't move on his behalf until instructed."

Henry couldn't speak. The heavenly being knew his thoughts. *I will do Your will Lord, not mine. Give me the strength and wisdom I need to advance Your kingdom.* Henry knelt for what felt like an eternity. No matter how many times he was brought to the top of the mountain, he dared not look directly into the heavenly being's eyes. Even though he was terrified in the moment, he felt renewed, refreshed, and strengthened afterwards. He knew the road ahead would be difficult, but as with everything timing was highly important. He opened his eyes and he was back among the trees outside his cabin. He got up with a bit of difficulty. His knees were not that of a young man anymore, but he knew God would give him what he needed until the day he went home for good.

Vickie sat on the couch with her eyes closed, taking in the sweet sensation of feeling lighter than air. She hadn't felt this good in a long time. Phil stroked her face gently. It felt comforting. She sighed. When she opened her eyes Phil's face was close up against hers. His stare satisfied her in a strange way.

"You're so beautiful." He took his index finger and outlined her lips, just like Sal did the night before. "I've missed those luscious lips of yours baby." Vickie felt as if she was watching this unfold from outside her body. He leaned in and she felt his wet lips on hers. His kiss was warm and familiar. He pulled her closer and she felt his hand reach up for her bra strap.

"Stop!" she managed to say. She pushed him away and stumbled up from the couch. "This was a bad idea. You have to go now. I don't want to see you again."

Laughing, Phil picked up the rest of his drugs, got up and walked towards her. "Sure, baby. Whatever you say, but that kiss says you're not over me. I'm a patient man 'cause I know you'll be back. You know where to find me and my *goodies*." He gave her a peck on her cheek.

She wiped it off as she watched him close the door. She walked over to lock it and caught a glimpse of herself in the mirror. *What's wrong with you?* She was disgusted with herself. The drugs made her not care. That kiss felt dirty, but how close she had come to letting herself get trapped in that life again disgusted her. Vickie made up her mind. She needed better self-control. She could do this, but she felt sick at the moment. She better sleep it off. She'll get Joey later. He's safe with the Delfenos.

Joey sat at Mrs. Delfeno's kitchen table as he dunked his warm chocolate chip cookie in the cold milk. He reached in with his fingers to gather the pieces that fell apart during the dunk.

"Then the princess had to choose which knight was worthy to win her hand. She decided she would hold a joust to help her decide."

"What's a *doust*, Mrs. D?" Joey interrupted.

Mrs. Delfeno looked up from her book, smiled at his pronunciation and answered, "It's when two knights on horses, with very long spears in their hands, ride their horses toward each other. Whoever gets knocked off their horse loses."

With eyes wide, Joey said, "Wow! Does he die?"

"No, Sweetie. The long spears have an end on it that doesn't hurt. It's just knocks down the other knight. The knights wear suits of armor that protect them."

"What's armor?"

Mrs. Delfeno smiled. "It's made of iron and it covers the knight's entire body like a suit."

Al walked into the kitchen and sat down next to his wife. He grabbed a cookie from the plate. "I couldn't help overhearing your story from the other room Marie. I can't wait to hear what happens next. What about you Joey?"

"Please, please read some more Mrs. D."

"Okay, you two. So then..." the doorbell interrupted her. "Al, go see who that is."

Al grinned and said, "Ah, man do I have to?"

"Now Al Delfeno, you behave."

"Okay, but you'll need to read me the rest of the story later?" he said with a wink.

"Only if you're a good boy," she replied.

Even after all these years together, he loved her flirtatious ways. Al heard Marie's voice in the background as she read to Joey. He loved how that little boy brought joy to his wife whenever he visited. He peeked through the peephole and didn't recognize the man he saw behind the door. He put the chain on as a precaution. He yelled without opening the door, "What do you want?"

"Could you open up sir? I just want to talk to you for a minute."

"Say your peace through the door." Al wasn't a fool. He wouldn't open up for a stranger.

"Okay then. I just thought you might want to know that I heard screaming coming from an apartment on the third floor. You might want to check it out. I think it's the apartment right above yours," the man said.

Al opened the door slightly with the chain still on as a safeguard. He watched the man as he left the building.

Marie entered the room with a scowl on her face. "Al, what's wrong?"

"It's okay honey. Go back and read to Joey. I'm going to check on Vickie." Al grabbed his master key chain from the hook by the door and headed for Vickie's apartment.

Al rang the doorbell. When there was no answer, he knocked. Still no response. *What if she's hurt?* Al opened the door slowly. "Mrs. Martinelli! Vickie! It's me, Mr. Delfeno." He looked around and saw feet sticking out of the doorframe of the kitchen. "Vickie!" He rushed over to her. He knelt down on the floor beside her. "Please wake up." She lay sprawled out on the floor in the kitchen, drool emanating from her mouth.

Sal found his front door opened. Panicked, he ran inside. "Vickie! Joey!" The sight of Mr. Delfeno kneeling next to Vickie's unconscious body caused his heart to miss a beat. "Mr. Delfeno! What's going on?"

"I don't know. Someone came to my door and said he heard a scream coming from your apartment. I rang the doorbell but when I didn't get an answer, I knocked. There was still no answer, so I came in." Mr. Delfeno made room for Sal. "I'll call for an ambulance."

"Where's Joey?"

"Don't worry, son. He's been downstairs with Marie. He doesn't know what happened."

Sal sighed. Relief washed over him. "Thank you. I'll take care of her. She'll be fine. I'll come down for Joey in a little bit." The scenario that lay before him was all too familiar. Embarrassed he continued, "Don't worry Mr. Delfeno. She's going to be okay." It was as if on cue, Vickie moaned. "I'll get her to bed. You can see yourself out, if you don't mind."

"Sure thing."

"Mr. Delfeno." He stopped and turned around. "There's no need to bother Mrs. Delfeno with any of this. You know how she tends to worry."

"Just between you and me."

"What's going on?" Vickie muttered as she started to come

around.

"You were passed out on the floor," Sal answered as he helped her to feet. She held on to him but her knees buckled. He helped her to the bedroom, laid her on her side, propped pillows to make sure she stayed that way, and lovingly covered her with the sheets. *Dear God, not again.*

"I'm sorry Sally. Don't be mad," she cried out.

"Shhhh. Go to sleep. We'll talk about this later."

He stood next to the bed as a tear slowly rolled down his cheek. Her breathing seemed to regulate itself again. He turned, walked out of the room and closed the door. He leaned against the bedroom door and sighed. He stood there in disbelief that Vickie would risk everything and start using drugs again. He knew who gave them to her and wondered what else was exchanged between them. *I better get Joey.*

Chapter 4

When Vickie opened her eyes, she had that all too familiar feeling. It hugged her as if it were a long lost-friend. She wished she were dead. She turned her head and saw Sal seated in the corner chair, eyes ablaze. "Hi," she whispered softly.

"Seriously? You let that man into our home again and all you can muster is 'hi'."

She tried to formulate the right words, "I... I... didn't invite him. He just showed up... You're right. I should have never opened up the door. I don't know what came over me." The look of hurt was more than Vickie could bear, but something inside of her couldn't stop playing with danger. Sal didn't respond, so she continued to ramble on, "I opened the door just so he wouldn't cause a scene with the neighbors, and he practically forced his way into the apartment. I don't know how he got past the front door. He must have snuck in with someone. I'm telling you the truth."

He cleared his throat, and then whispered, "The truth? I don't believe you ever met the word. Your mouth moves and nothing but lies come sailing out of it."

Vickie got up and knelt by Sal with her hands on his knees. "I swear on my mother's grave, I'm not lying."

"You need help. I can't have you around Joey if you're doing drugs again. I love you, Vickie, but..."

"But what? You're so perfect to live with. You never make a mistake? Just because I had a little slip, doesn't mean I'm a bad mother. You're being unfair," she whined. Desperation fueled her.

"Unfair?" Sal lost his temper and stood up. "Did you sleep with him *this time?*"

"Wow!... Your opinion of me is low," she said wounded by his words.

"That doesn't answer my question." She's seen him angry before, but he seemed to have slipped into indifference. This would not bode well for her.

"No, I didn't. You have to believe me. I didn't do that."

"You're a drug addict... I can't trust you. Every time I do, you disappoint me. We've been around this mountain too many times to count. I sat here watching you and realized I'm just tired of it. I told you the last time, that would be the last time. No more chances. Joey is almost five. He needs and deserves a mother who won't pass out on him. He needs someone who puts him first. What he doesn't need is a selfish, slutty drug addict who only thinks of her next fix."

His harsh words felt like a knife cutting her flesh, but he wasn't wrong in his assessment. "I guess I deserved that, but I didn't sleep with him."

"You mean *this* time."

"Yeah, *this* time," she paused. "Please. I'll do whatever you want. I'll go to whatever program you want. Please. I beg you... think about Joey. I'll do anything not to lose you both." Vickie's panic fell on deaf ears.

Sal's heart grew harder as the conversation continued. How many times had he heard her empty promises? How many times had he come home to find her passed out in her own vomit and Joey crying? How many times *did* she go to rehab? How many times could he put up with her cheating on him for drugs? He decided this was the last time. He looked at her coldly, void of love or compassion. "It's too late, Vickie. I've packed your clothes and your bag is by the door. I'm calling a lawyer." As the words came out of his mouth, Sal wanted to take them back, but he needed to be strong. Tough love was the only thing left.

"I've got no where to go."

"You can go to rehab or you can go back to your drug pushing boyfriend. You seem to care more for him than your family. Either way, I'm done."

Sobbing, she crawled over to where he stood, "Sal, please, please, please don't do this. I promise I'll be good. Nothing happened with Phil." Sal couldn't look at her as she spoke. He felt it would kill him. "Okay, you're right. I let him in. He just wanted to talk. He took out the drugs and I... I had a weak moment. He tried to kiss me, but that was the only thing that happened."

He felt as if he fell into a black hole. "Keep your voice down! Joey is in the other room." Speaking in a low, steady voice he continued, "I'm going to take him out to eat and I want you gone by the time we get back. Is that clear?"

"Sal... please." She grabbed his legs.

He pushed her hands off his legs. "Is that clear?" he repeated.

"Yeah," she said as her head hung down.

Before he left, he turned around and said, "One more thing." She looked up at him. "I want you to leave your key." He slammed the door on his way out.

Sal smiled as Joey struggled to hold his slice of pizza in his hands. He refused having his pizza cut in half. He wanted to eat like a grown up—folded in half. His happiness was what mattered. Sal chose to be focused on the good in his life. *Was it really over?* "Are you enjoying your pizza, Bud?"

"Yeah! It's cheesy," he said as he took another bite. Suddenly with saddened eyes Joey asked, "How come Mommy couldn't come Daddy? She loves pizza too."

"This is our special Daddy and son time," he lied. He took a deep breath and continued, "Joey. I have something to tell you." Joey looked up at him. "Your Mommy is going on a trip again."

"Is she going to come back soon?"

"I'm sorry son, not this time. This will be a long trip and I'm not sure how long she will be gone."

Joey pushed his slice away. "I'm not hungry anymore, Daddy."

Reaching for his little hand, "Don't be sad, Bud. It's going to be okay. I promise I will take good care of you... You start school next week. Aren't you excited about that?"

"Mommy was going to buy stuff for school."

"What if I take you and you can pick out what you like. You'll see we'll make a day of it. We can go tomorrow."

"Okay, Daddy."

"Now finish up your pizza slice. We'll stop at the store and get you some candy."

"Yeah!!! I love candy."

"Of course you do. You're my son."

The memory of Sal's father came to his mind. He always knew what the right thing to do was. He recalled when his mother died; he was only six years old...

"Hey there champ," Joseph said as he sat next to his son on the bed.

Sal didn't look up. He was holding the only picture he had of his mother—Sal as a baby in his mother's arms. Tears soaked his face.

"You know that your Mommy loved you very much."

"Then why did she leave?"

Joseph lifted his face by his chin. "Sal, she didn't want to leave. She got sick. She tried to stay, but heaven really needed her. She's an angel watching over you and me now."

"I don't want heaven to have her. I need her more."

Joseph looked at his son. Sal noticed, even at that age, his father's eyes watered. "I know you'll miss her, but she'll never be very far. She'll always live inside your heart and mine. She told me right before she left to take care of you. She wanted to make sure you knew how much she loved you."

"I don't know how to do that, Daddy. How do you remember someone in your heart?"

Joseph paused before he answered. "I'm not sure son, but will you do me a favor?"

Sal looked up at his father. "Sure, Daddy."

"Will you help me not to miss her too much? My heart hurts too. I think if we can talk about her and remember all the fun times we had, we'll be able to remember her in our hearts."

His dad was such a wise man. He missed him. He wondered what he would advise him to do about Vickie.

Vickie was shocked by Sal's reaction. *Why should you be?* She'd seen him cold and unfeeling a couple of times, but he seemed to have gone to a new level. It's not like she killed anyone or even slept with Phil this time. It was a momentary slip. It doesn't mean she's a drug addict again. She took her cell phone out of her pocket and dialed. "Yeah. It's me. I need a favor."

From the outside of the building, Vickie took one more look up at her apartment. As her eyes came down, she saw Mrs. Delfeno at her window. She got into Phil's car and as she shut the door she felt total hopelessness.

"Hey baby, why so glum? Now we can be together. That's the way it should be."

"Phil, let me be clear. This has nothing to do with you and me getting back together. It's just I... well, I've got nowhere else to go. I'm going to be sleeping on your couch until Sal cools off."

"Sure baby, whatever you say."

"I'm serious, Phil. You can wipe that stupid grin off your face now!" Vickie's words were strong, but she wasn't sure if Sal was ever going to calm down or if she could truly stay clean. She had to try. She didn't have any other friends. Phil might not be a friend, but she had no one else to turn to. *How sad was that?* "Remember you promised not to tempt me or have any stuff around me while I'm there."

"Scout's honor," he said while he did the three-fingered salute.

"You're no Boy Scout."

"I promise none the same."

"Phil, I'm serious. When Sal shows up I have to be clean or else I'll lose him forever."

"And this would be a bad thing?"

Vickie rolled her eyes. "Phil, stop the car!" Phil pulled over. "You promise me for real now or else…"

"Or else what? Come on, I promised already. Don't get so excited."

Vickie sighed. "I know I go back and forth about my feelings for Sal… I do love him… in my own way. He's a good dad, and Joey deserves that."

"Is that why you chose him or was it just your lucky day that he found you on that park bench?"

"Shut up. You promised never to talk about that. Sal's name is on the birth certificate and that's all I'm ever going to say about it!"

"Okay, okay. I'll take you to my place now." Phil made the gesture that his lips were sealed.

Chapter 5

Sal sat in the last row of Holy Trinity Church. Brokenhearted he looked up at the cross in the front of the church. Silently he prayed: *God I don't understand. Why doesn't she love me? Why can't she stay away from that man? What am I doing wrong?*

He wasn't sure how much time passed when he noticed Rose sitting on the opposite side of the aisle in the same row. Her eyes were closed with tear-stained cheeks. He wondered if she had been there the whole time. He wasn't sure if he should disturb her. If he was honest with himself he felt drawn to her—to her pain. Before he knew what he was doing, he stood next to the pew.

"Rose..."

She wiped the tears from her face, cleared her throat, then responded softly, "Hmm... hi."

"Are you alright?" he asked even though it was apparent she was not.

"I must look a mess."

"No... you don't."

"Liar." She took a tissue from her purse, tilted her head, "Today is the anniversary of Duane's death... I... I... just miss him."

"I'm so sorry to hear that Rose. Hey, there's a Starbuck's down the street. Do you want to have coffee? We can talk about it if you want." Rose didn't answer right away so Sal added, "I'm a good listener."

"I don't know..." She blew her nose. Even then, she was dignified and ladylike. "I guess it would be nice to talk to someone but... I'm buying."

"I don't think so. My dad would come back from the grave to haunt me if I let a lady pay for coffee."

Rose's smile brightened her complexion. She was absolutely beautiful in that moment.

Vickie sat on Phil's couch. She'd been camped out on his couch for the last couple of days. She'd called Sal every day and asked him if she could come home, but he refused when he found out she was with Phil. What did he expect? She didn't know anyone else. The only family she had was Sal and Joey. This vicious cycle she found herself in was her own doing. She needed time to think. Vickie was surprised by how much she missed her family. Phil kept his word, but if this arrangement extended much longer, she wasn't sure if she wouldn't falter.

"Hey, baby. Are you hungry?"

"No."

"You want something to make you feel better?" Phil said as he sat down next to her.

"No!"

Phil took out a plastic bag of white powder. "Are you sure?" he said as he shook it in front of her. She ignored him. "Why are you here then?"

"Because of you I needed a place to stay. Your visit got me thrown out."

"No... your being passed out when your husband got home got you thrown out." She couldn't argue with the facts.

"Besides, I'm not running a free hotel here, baby. How are you going to pay for all the food you've been eating and this comfortable couch you've been sleeping on?" He smirked.

What had she ever seen in him? Granted he had the looks of a movie star and a Svengali charm that made you believe anything he said, but underneath there was no substance. When she left Indiana, Phil was the first person she met. She already had emotional scars from her childhood. He seemed to understand her.

Since she kept silent, Phil continued, "All I'm saying is that it's costing me money having you here, not to mention it's cramping my style. I gotta get a little something, something if you know what I'm saying." Phil leaned in close and blew in her ear.

Vickie rolled her eyes. "I'm done. I'd rather sleep on a park bench then spend another day here with you." She started to gather her things. He didn't look that good to her when she was sober.

"What, you can't tell when I'm joking? We're old friends. You can stay—no strings attached."

Vickie ignored him and continued to pack her bag.

"Come on. Don't get mad. I said I was just kidding." He tried to reach out to her but she pulled away. "Stop!" She scowled at him.

"I'm sorry Vick. Are you hungry?" She didn't answer him. "How about I order some Chinese from that place that you like so much?" He paused. "Come on, Vick. Don't be so sensitive. You know it's a dangerous world out there. A pretty little thing like you wouldn't be safe on a park bench."

The ugly truth hit her as if she just jumped into Lake Placid in the middle of winter. She'd never felt more pathetic. "I guess you're right." Hopelessness fell on her like a cloak of darkness. She was consumed by it.

"When are you going to learn that old Phil is always right?"

Starbuck's was busy that time of day. Sal and Rose sat in the corner on some oversized chairs. The noise didn't disrupt their conversation. It was as if they were the only people in the room.

"Thank you, Sal."

"For what?"

"For listening. I've been doing so well until today. I'm so glad you were at the church." Rose brow raised and she continued, "I've been boring you about my troubles for the past hour."

"You weren't boring me." They smiled at one another.

"I know why I was there, but why were you at the church?"

"Do you remember the first time we had coffee at Starbuck's?" He changed the subject.

Rose blushed. She remembered all too well that first blind date she had with him. "I thought you promised to never speak of that again."

"Oh come on, you were adorable."

"Adorable. Is that what you call my sweating—adorable."

He chuckled but continued, "Well, maybe it was the toilet paper that was stuck on your neck that was adorable."

"It's not my fault it was so humid on that day or that the air conditioning was broken and blew hot air instead of cold. I wanted to make a good impression and... I didn't want my shirt to get wet. When I tried to dry off in the bathroom there were no paper towels. By that time my shirt was soaked. It wasn't easy trying to dry it off under the hand dryer. It made me sweat more. I had no idea the toilet paper was stuck on the back of my neck."

Sal smiled.

"I see what you're doing."

"Is it working?" he asked.

"No... What where you doing at the church today?"

Sal's expression changed. "I was trying to seek guidance... I threw my wife out of the house a few days ago."

It sounded harsh, but the Sal Rose remembered must have had a good reason. "Is there a chance you two can work it out?"

"I'm not sure. There's a huge mountain we keep going around. I have to think about Joey. She's just not fit to be around him in her... condition."

Rose felt compelled to ask, "What condition?"

He blurted, "She's a drug addict who sleeps around with her supplier." Rose sensed the hurt of his words and saw the pain in his eyes.

She reached over and touched his hand. "I'm so sorry." *Come on Rose, you can do better than that.* She felt her heartstrings tug when she felt the warmth of his hand. He looked at her. His soft brown eyes penetrated her soul.

"Joey is having a hard time with his mother being gone."

Rose stroked his arm. "The children always have the toughest time with separation. I'm sorry you're going through such a rough patch. I'm sure it will work out."

"I'm not as sure as you are, but thanks for your encouragement." He paused. Her heartbeat quickened. She knew she had to go home. She wasn't sure if she had the strength needed to do the right thing.

"It's getting late," she said quickly as she withdrew her hand from his arm.

"Yeah... um, I gotta get Joey."

"Thanks for listening, Sal. You're a good friend."

"No problem. It was good to have a nonjudgmental ear to talk to."

Rose stood up. "Well, I've gotta catch the bus."

"The bus?"

"Yeah... my car is in the shop."

"That's silly. I'll drive you home."

Rose thought about that for a moment and against her better judgment she replied, "Okay, thanks."

Phil came through the door like he just won the lottery. "What are you so happy about? Did you trip the delivery man?" she asked.

"Ah, that's what I missed most about you Vick—your charming, sarcastic wit."

"Bite me!"

"Really?" Phil replied with an eyebrow raised.

"Pig."

"All this sweet talk will give a guy the wrong idea." He placed the bags on the table. "Can you get some plates and napkins?"

"Fine," she mumbled.

He watched her leave the room. He took the containers out of the bag. He opened a few until he found the beef lo mien, Vickie's favorite. He opened up a couple of capsules and emptied the contents into the food and stirred it around with a chopstick.

Vickie entered, placing the plates and napkins on the table. They sat down and started to put food on their plates.

Sal and Rose stood in front of her door. She looked longingly in his eyes. *What are you doing, Sal? If you take this to the next step, then there's no difference between you and Vickie.* Sal took a step back. "Rose... I can't be anything but a friend to you right now. My life is so complicated," he said as he swallowed hard.

"I've never said I wanted anything more from you than friendship. What kind of woman do you think I am?" she protested.

"I... I... I wasn't trying to imply you were... I'm sorry. I better go now." He turned around.

"Sal, wait. I'm sorry. I didn't mean to... it's been a hard day and you've been so kind."

"I didn't mean to suggest... ugh... I'm a jerk sometimes and apparently a little bit full of myself."

Rose giggled. "No sweat. Um... if I hug you goodbye would you think I wanted to marry you?"

Sal shook his head. "I guess I deserve that." He embraced her. He felt her warmth throughout his body. "Can I see you again?"

"Sure. Give me a call." Rose's smile filled the entire hallway with light, or was it just his imagination?

Sal couldn't get to his car fast enough. He felt attracted to Rose but he still loved Vickie. That was the problem. He accused her of what was in his own heart to do. He sat there, and pondered what might have just happened if he had acted on his feelings for Rose. He assumed Rose would have been a willing participant. Maybe he sensed something from her, or maybe it was all in his lonely imagination. He felt the urge to see Vickie. Maybe he should just go get Vickie and give her one more chance for Joey's sake. She left messages assuring him nothing was going on. Maybe he should just show up there and see for himself.

Vickie stared at her food. She wasn't really hungry. She felt as if something was wrong but couldn't place her finger on it. Her throat was tight and fear started to overtake her.

"You haven't touched your food, Vick."

"I'm not hungry. I think I just want to go home now."

"I thought you didn't have a home to go to," Phil said as he took a bite of his food. "Why don't just take just a few bites. I bought your favorite."

"Yeah, you're right." Defeated she was about to take a bite when the doorbell rang. "You want me to get that?"

"No. I'll get it." Phil looked through the peephole. Cursing beneath his breath, he opened the door. "Well, well looky here, if it ain't Mr. I Threw My Wife Out Because I'm A Self-Righteous Bastard."

Vickie jumped from the table and ran to the door. "Sal!" She was excited to see him.

Sal walked past Phil and extended his hand toward Vickie. "Where are your things?"

"I'm already packed. It's by the couch, where I've been sleeping."

Sal smiled and grabbed her bag with one hand and Vickie's hand with the other. Without saying another word to Phil, they both walked out.

Chapter 6

Rose sat on her couch deep in thought. Her apartment was modest. Minimalist was a better term to excuse her lack of décor. In the corner of the living room a lonely, half dead plant sat on a small table along with a picture of Duane. The picture was taken on their honeymoon in Hawaii. She loved his smile in that photo. They had had such a good time together. The couch she had bought from a secondhand store was a throwback from the seventies, but was in good shape. The lamps were a present from her mother. The built-in bookcases stood empty. Most of her things were still in the spare room. She couldn't bear the thought of sifting through her life with Duane. It was a year later, but the pain she experienced felt fresh.

A twinge of guilt filled her emptiness. Who would have thought after all these years old feelings would resurface for Sal. It didn't work out the first time around, and now he was married, period. She knew better. She didn't want to confuse his kindness for anything else. The doorbell interrupted her thoughts. She opened it to find a pleasant surprise.

"Mom! What brings you here?"

Lauren Satin didn't appear her sixty years. Her hair was as red as it ever was and her skin flawless. She swore she never colored it and attributed her youthful appearance to good genes. Often she was mistaken for Rose's sister, a mistake Lauren relished. "I was in the neighborhood."

"Really now? You're in the neighborhood with a plate of my favorite cookies."

Lauren laughed. "Okay, you got me. I dropped off your sister at a friend's house, and thought I would visit with you for a while if you're not busy."

"I'm never too busy for you, Mom. Come in," Rose said as she took the plate of cookies from her mom. "Just say it."

"What do you mean honey?"

"I can tell by the look on your face you don't approve of my decor or should I say the lack of it."

Lauren sighed. "Honey, it's just... it's been a year. There comes a time when you need to move forward. You're holed up in here, except for when you go to work or I invite you over."

Rose couldn't help it, she rolled her eyes as if she was still in high school. "Mom, really I'm okay. Just because I'm not out partying doesn't mean I'm not moving forward with my life. My job keeps me very busy. I also go to church."

"How about some coffee?" her mother asked. "I'll make my special blend. I happen to have some in my purse." Lauren shifted through her giant bag and pulled out a bag of coffee.

"Of course you do. What else do you have in there?"

"Mock me if you wish, but I can't help it... I'm a mom, and we're always prepared."

Henry and Ida got out of the taxicab. The driver helped them with their bags, and carried them to the front door. Henry gave him a modest tip.

"Who says New Yorkers are rude? That young man was simply delightful, wasn't he, Henry?"

"Yes, Ida, he was."

The door opened before Henry could knock. A beautiful brunette answered the door. Her smile lit up his heart. She hugged him and smiled at Ida. "You must be Ida," she said before Henry said a word of introduction and quickly embraced her.

"This has been one the friendliest places I've ever been to. You're even more beautiful than Henry described."

"Come in you two. You must be tired after your flight." She

grabbed their bags, placed them inside. She walked into the living room where her son was playing with blocks. "Michael, come and say hello to our guests."

He looked up from his blocks, "Hello. I'm *tree* years old and my baby sista *Irca* is *sick* months old," he said with excitement.

"You mean six months old? He still has trouble saying *Erica*."

"Yeah, six... months... old. Would you like to see my room?" he said without missing a beat.

"I would love to." Ida smiled from ear to ear.

"You don't have to do that right now. Why don't you have a seat? Michael, you can show Mrs. James your room later."

"No dear, I don't mind. This gives you and Henry a chance to catch up. Okay, young man, let's see this special room of yours." Grabbing Ida's hand Michael pulled her toward his room.

"Don't fret. Ida loves kids more than anything else. So, how are you and John?"

"We're great. He's such an exceptional father. He treats Michael like his own son and is totally in love with Erica. He asked me to apologize that he couldn't be here to greet you because he had to work."

"No need for apologies. I know he's busy keeping the city safe. We'll have plenty of time to catch up later."

"Would you like some tea or something else to drink? Are you hungry?" Her words spilled out with excitement.

"Please, sit, dear. I'm just fine. I'm very happy to see that life is kind to you both. God is good."

"Yes, He is... Henry, tell me more about what brings you here?"

"It's a young man. I'm afraid he has a hard road ahead of him. I need to stay close until the right time. It's very kind of you and John to open your home to us. I promise not to be a burden."

"You could never be a burden. After what you did for us, you and Ida are welcome to stay as long as you need."

"I can't take any credit for that."

"That's because you're humble. You were the willing vessel that He used."

"I have friends, Mom!" Rose said a bit more forcefully than she intended.

Lauren took a sip of her coffee. Rose felt her stare as it burned a hole through her. "Having coffee with your married ex-boyfriend doesn't count, Rose."

Her mother's words stung more than she wanted to reveal at the moment. "Thanks for the coffee, Mom... and the cookies. I really need to get back to this project I have to do for work." She opened the front door as her mom gathered her things. "Give Candy my love, and tell her to stop by sometime."

At the door, Lauren brushed Rose's hair from her eyes as if she were still a little girl. "I love you, Rose. I don't want to see you get hurt. You've been through so much. Don't set yourself up for more pain."

"I'm not. We're just friends."

Lauren kissed her on the cheek and walked out the door. Rose closed the door while tears ran down her face. She slid against the door and sat on the floor. Maybe her mom was right. Her relationship with Sal must stay on the friendship level. *Dear God, help me to stay pure of heart and mind. Let me be a friend to Sal and nothing more. Help me be a true friend and not another source of concern.* She took her cell phone out of her pocket and dialed his number. It rang four times before going to voicemail. "Hello, Sal. I just wanted to apologize again for any misunderstandings today. Truly, my heart is to just be a friend to you. I know I certainly can use one right about now. Maybe we can have coffee again and talk... Well anyway, have a great day." She hung up and spoke out loud, "Boy, that was the dumbest message I have ever left on anyone's voicemail. I should have just left well enough alone. *'Have a great day?'* *What a lame thing to say.*

Nadine Zawacki

Chapter 7

Vickie watched from the doorway of Joey's room as Sal read a bedtime story to him.

"And they lived happily ever after. The end."

"How come they always live happily ever after, Daddy?"

"I guess it makes for a nice story, Joey. People like a happy ending. Now it's time for you to close your eyes and sleep."

"I love you, Daddy." Sal kissed him on the forehead. "I love you, Mommy." Vickie walked in to deliver her goodnight kiss.

"I love you too, little man. We'll see you in the morning."

"I'm happy you're home, Mommy."

"I'm happy to be home."

Closing the door halfway, Vickie followed Sal into their bedroom. He sat at the edge of the bed staring at her. *Why doesn't he say something?* He hadn't spoken much since he had picked her up. Clearing her throat, "Do you want me to sleep on the couch?" Silence. "You have every right to be mad. I screwed up, again." *I wish he would say anything... scream or yell.* "But you threw me out, remember?" All she saw was a blank look on his face. "I had nowhere else to go... Nothing happened while I was there. I didn't snort coke or sleep with Phil. I swear!" Vickie watched as a tear fell down his cheek. "I'm sorry, Sal. I always seem to hurt you." Still he didn't utter a word. "You're too good for me. I don't deserve you."

"I'm sorry for throwing you out. I made a promise to love you in sickness and in health until death do us part." Sal's cell phone rang, but Vickie decided not to make an issue of it.

"You can answer that if you need to."

"Whoever it is can wait." He rose from the bed and didn't remove his eyes from hers. Vickie couldn't look at him anymore and just lowered her eyes to the floor. She felt his gentle touch on her face. Goosebumps ran down her arm. When he stroked her hair it comforted her in a weird way. *How can any drug compare to what I'm feeling right now? Why?... Why can't this feeling last?*

"Look at me," he said softly. She looked in his eyes. Her guilt engulfed her as tears filled the corner of her eyes. She felt his hands around her waist. He pulled her close and kissed her. His kiss filled her with passion that buckled her knees. She was taken aback when her thoughts drifted toward Phil. She remembered *his* kiss and *his* touch. Her body responded passionately to her imagination. He lifted her in his arms and placed her on the bed. Her mind drifted back and forth from Phil to Sal. She was swept up in the moment. *What he doesn't know... right?*

Sal hadn't slept that well in weeks. It felt good to make love to his wife with such passionate abandon. He rolled over and watched as she slept. He glanced at the clock and realized it was time for him to get up for work. The last thing Sal wanted was to leave the comfort of his warm bed. He never felt more in love with her than at that moment. So he kissed her gently on the cheek and hoped it would awaken her and it did. "Hey, sleepy head. It's time to get up."

"'Morning."

"I'm going to jump in the shower," Sal said as he kissed gently on her lips.

"I'll start breakfast."

"Don't go to any trouble."

"It's no trouble."

Sal watched as Vickie got out of bed. She put on her robe, turned and smiled. He was pleased with himself. *Maybe this time things will be different.* Sal turned the water on and stepped into the shower. The warm water felt good against his skin. It felt as if the last six years were washed from his mind, body and soul. He started to sing, "Shake Your Groove Thing."

"Hey, Peaches!" Vickie's voice startled him. He heard her chuckle. "Do you mind keeping it down? Joey is still asleep."

"Sorry, baby. I'm just in a very good mood. For the record, I was 'Herb' not 'Peaches.'"

"Yeah, yeah. Whatever. Keep it down."

Sal stuck his head through the shower curtain. "How about you joining me in here?"

"Didn't get enough last night? I must be slipping."

"It's lonely in here," he whined.

"Rain check. I'm in the middle of breakfast. It'll be ready in fifteen minutes, so hurry up."

"Party pooper."

Henry felt troubled. He rose from the bed and knelt down beside it. "Father, something ain't right. I pray right now that You be with that young man. Give him the strength he will need to stand firm in You. Amen." Henry left Ida asleep in the bed and went out to the kitchen. He smiled when he saw Regina. "Good morning. That coffee sure smells good."

"Well, there's a cup with your name on it." She poured him a cup. "Did you sleep well? You look a bit tired."

"The accommodations were wonderful... I guess you can say there was a disturbance in the force. I'm afraid that young man is about to face a whole world of pain."

"Anything I can do?"

"Just pray for him."

Sal's exuberant joy added to Vickie's guilt about the night before. It was one of their more passionate nights together, but it wasn't real... at least not for her. Joey's voice shook her from her fog.

"Good morning, Mommy. Did you make eggs? I love eggs."

"Yes, I did. Here you go, honey. Scrambled just the way you like them. Now sit down. After breakfast, we'll go out to the mall to get some supplies for school."

"I already got them, Mommy. Daddy took me."

"Oh. That's fine. How about we go to the zoo? Next week school starts, and I won't have as much time with you."

"Yeah!! The zoo! I love the zoo!"

"Morning, Buddy. You sound very excited." Sal patted him on his head.

"Mommy is taking me to the zoo. Can you come, Daddy?"

"I wish I could, but I have to go to the store today. I'm sure you will have a great time with your Mommy."

"Here are your eggs, Sal." He kissed her on her cheek.

"Yum. Sunnyside up just the way I like them." He gave her a hug around her waist. Vickie resisted the urge to pull away. In the morning light things felt different.

"Since everything is under control here, why don't you guys enjoy your breakfast while I get cleaned up."

Vickie walked into the bedroom, relieved to be alone. Her thoughts betrayed her. A hot shower would definitely help. Before entering the bathroom, she noticed Sal had left his cell phone on the nightstand. As she picked it up to bring it to him, she remembered that it rang last night. Curiosity got the better of her. She saw the voicemail was from someone named Rose Wells. *Didn't he date a Rose right before they met?*

"Who's Rose Wells?"

"Oh, Vickie, I didn't even hear you come back into the kitchen."

"I'll ask again, who's Rose Wells?"

"She's an old friend from college."

"An old friend? You mean *that* Rose?" She held up the phone, "You left this in the bedroom. Looks like she left a message. Shall we listen to what *your friend* has to say?"

"Vickie. Wait. It's not what you think. We ran into each other at church. She just lost her husband and we talked over coffee."

"Joey. Why don't you go to your room and get dressed."

"Grown-up talk," he said as he left the room.

Vickie waited until Joey left the room and then pressed play:

"Hi, Sal. I just wanted to apologize again for any misunder-standings today. Truly, my heart is to just be a friend to you. I know I certainly can use one right about now. Maybe we can have coffee again and talk... Well anyway, have a great day."

"Yeah, that's exactly what that sounds like—just coffee," she said sarcastically.

Nadine Zawacki

Chapter 8

Rose entered the candy story a lot noisier than she anticipated. She hadn't realized there was a bell on the door that chimed when someone entered. A sales lady placed what looked like gummy bears in a jar on a shelf. She smiled widely and said, "Good morning."

"Hello... I'm... um... looking for... "

"Well, no matter what you're looking for dear, we probably have it, and if we don't, I know where to get it. The one thing Mr. Martinelli likes is variety." She smiled again.

Rose started again, "Um... that's good to know but... um... I'm looking for... Mr. Martinelli. Is he here?" Rose felt awkward when the sales lady gave her the once over with her eyes.

"He's in his office. Whom shall I say is looking for him?"

"I'm an old friend from college. My name is Rose."

"Rose? As in the Rose he broke up with in college?" This woman knew a lot. Rose didn't hide her displeasure.

"Excuse me. I don't think that should matter to his *sales girl* who I am?"

Pausing before she spoke, "Apologies dear. I think of Sal as much more than an employer. We're also friends. I tend to speak my mind without much of a filter. No disrespect was intended."

Rose was now self-conscious. "It's okay. I was being too sensitive." Rose paused and continued, "I'm sorry for the *sales girl* crack, that was totally uncalled for."

"I'll get him."

Vickie thought Joey was going to pull her arm out of the socket. He was so excited to be at the zoo. His favorite part was the petting section. "Mommy, can I feed the animals?"

"Give the lady this money, and she'll give you food for the animals. Be careful now."

"What a cute son you have." A familiar voice spoke from behind her.

Vickie turned slowly. "Phil." She had a hard time hiding her disgust.

"Don't be that way, baby. You know you're happy to see me."

"Why do you always lick your lips when you're around me? It's disgusting."

"Because you're yummy." With one eyebrow raised and a crooked smile Phil continued, "Look. The way it ended with you and me—not cool. You know this domestic diva crap doesn't suit you."

Vickie had a hard time coming up with an argument, especially when she considered her fantasies the night before. Why does she let him get under her skin? She walked toward Joey. "Just leave. I'm here with my kid. I don't want you around him."

"*Your* kid?"

"What do you mean by that?"

"Oh baby, don't play coy with me. It doesn't suit you."

Vickie knew where he was headed. She didn't like it. "We've been over this a million times."

"Yeah, I know... but, no matter how many times you say a lie..."

"Enough! Not here!... Not now," she yelled louder than intended.

"Okay." Phil walked over to Joey. He stooped down to Joey's level. "Hi there, Joey. I'm a friend of your Mommy's. Would you like some ice cream?"

Joey looked up at his mother. He asked, "Can I, Mommy? I love ice cream."

Vickie didn't like to disappoint her son, especially when he looked at her with those big hazel eyes of his. She nodded her approval and watched closely as he took Phil's hand and walked toward the ice cream stand. Visions of last night kept going through her mind. With all her might she tried to stop them. Suddenly the phone message from Rose revisited her thoughts. Sure, he came up with some lame excuse that made it sound all innocent, but he had some nerve "going out" with another woman, especially that one. *Why am I mad? I've done worse than just have coffee.* Justification crept into her mind and pushed all logic out. She felt anger replace logic in her thoughts. The more she thought about Rose, anger's little brothers joined in—resentment and bitterness. *That man just ticks me off. Well, if he can be friends with his "ex," then so can I.*

"So, Phil, do I get an ice cream treat too?"

Phil smiled from ear to ear and gave her a wink, "Sure, anything for a friend."

"Afternoon, Rose. It's good to see you." Sal couldn't help but notice Margaret's uncomfortable stare. "Margaret, could you finish checking the inventory for me?" he said as he handed her his clipboard.

"You're the boss," Margaret replied as she left for the back room. He loved that Margaret cared for him, but she'd read more into the situation than warranted.

"What brings you here today, Rose?"

"I… um… felt weird about how we left things and then… um… I left you that stupid message… oh boy… I'm sorry; this was a bad idea."

"You have nothing to be sorry for. We can be friends can't we?"

"Yes… friends… That's exactly what I need right now. Well then, since we cleared that up. I guess I can go now."

Sal watched as she walked toward the door. He stilled cared about her. He saw the pain in her eyes, and compassion rose inside of him. "Wait. You don't have to go yet, do you?... I mean you've not been in here before. Take a look around, and you can have anything you want... on the house of course."

Her eyes sparkled. It made Sal remember why they were together in college. Those eyes always made his heart stop. She was a beautiful woman with bright green eyes that accented her red hair. Why did he break up with her? Oh yeah... Vickie.

"I do love chocolate, and you could twist my arm to take some home with me," Rose said with a smile.

Margaret cleared her throat as she entered. "I'm all done, Boss." She only called him that when she was upset with him.

"Thanks, Margaret."

"You know on second thought, I should be going. I have some errands to run before dinner with my mom. It was nice seeing you again, Sal. I'll take a rain check on the chocolates."

As she grabbed the handle, Sal yelled out, "Caramel filled chocolate still your favorite?"

She stopped, turned. "Yeah. It's still my favorite." Rose smiled bashfully.

Sal had a hard time hiding the grin on his face. He turned to find Margaret still standing there. She looked around, but not at him directly. "Go ahead. Say it. You know you want to."

"I've got nothing to say, Boss."

"Oh, yes, you do. And do me a favor; stop calling me Boss."

Sal watched Margaret's eyes as they roamed the room as if she was searching for words to magically appear in the atmosphere. "It's none of my business, but since you asked... when someone is having trouble in their marriage, reconnecting with a past love is not very bright."

"Don't hold back, Margaret."

"She's very pretty."

"That has nothing to do with it. We're just friends. She recently lost her husband, and I was just trying to be..."

"To be what... his replacement?"

"Hey, I thought you knew me better than that," he said, irritated.

"Not saying you would, dear boy; just saying that temptations can sometimes prove overwhelming even to good men like yourself. I don't want to see you get hurt. I couldn't care for you more than if you were my son."

"I know you do, Margaret. But you don't have to worry. I'm not going to get hurt. You're a good lady that I care about deeply. Your heart is in the right place, but I'll say it again: we're just friends."

"Friends."

"Yeah, friends."

"Do the math, Sal—two people plus pain equals trouble."

"You're wrong about this, Margaret."

"Okay, it wouldn't be the first time I was wrong. Know that I'm here for you. That's all I'm going to say on the matter."

Sal doubted very much if that was the last he would hear from Margaret, but she dropped the subject for now, and for that he was grateful.

Nadine Zawacki

Chapter 9

When Vickie entered the apartment building she wasn't surprised to see Mrs. Delfeno outside her door. "Good afternoon," she said with a big smile on her face when she saw Joey.

"Mrs. D, guess what?"

"What?"

"Mommy took me to the zoo today. I gave baby animals food. They ate out of my hand. Mommy's friend got us ice cream! It was fun."

"Well how nice of your Mommy's friend to buy you ice cream."

"We'll see you later. I have to get dinner together before Sal gets home. Say good-bye to Mrs. Delfeno, Joey."

"Good-bye, Mrs. D. See ya."

"I can't wait to hear all about the zoo. Maybe tomorrow we can visit over some of my home-made cookies."

"Yeah! Can I Mommy?"

"We'll see." She wanted to usher Joey away. What if he had told her the friend's name or that it was a man?

They walked up instead of waiting for the slow elevator. Vickie didn't realize that Mrs. Delfeno was listening to their conversation at the bottom of the stairs. "Now Joey, you don't have to tell that woman everything that happened today. Remember we talked about keeping the ice cream part a secret."

"I thought it was a secret from Daddy. I'm sorry Mommy."

"That's okay. You didn't do anything wrong. We just don't want Daddy to get upset because he wanted to come to the zoo with us. He would feel bad that he wasn't the one who bought you ice cream."

"I remember. Can I tell him about the elephants?"

"Of course you can, just not about Mommy's friend."

She opened the door to their apartment. "Go play in your room while I make dinner, okay baby."

"Mommy, I'm no baby. I'm going to school next week." Vickie closed the door behind them.

"That's right little man. Now go." Vickie's cell phone rang. *Should I answer?* "Phil, you have to stop calling me."

"Hey, baby. I miss you."

"We spent the afternoon together. What do you want?

"What I always want... you."

"Well you can't always get what you want."

"So cold Vickie... you wound me."

"Shut up, Phil."

"I had a great time with you and Joey. That kid has the most interesting eyes, don't you think?"

"Yeah! Mine!"

"You know how good we were together once. Do you remember how exciting life was and how I made you feel when I..."

"Enough! I gotta go." With that she ended the call and placed it in her pocket. Phil called again, but she didn't answer. She had to be strong. Dinner won't make itself. She mindlessly started dinner. Vickie wasn't sure how much time passed, when she heard...

"I'm home." Sal walked into the kitchen. "Hey, beautiful."

"Hey, yourself." He kissed her. "How was your day?" she asked.

"Good. How was the zoo?"

"Good. Joey had a great time. Anything interesting happen at the store?"

"No... Slow day... Did inventory. It's all good."

Joey ran into the room to greet his father. "Daddy's home!! Yeah!"

"Hey, Bud. Did you have fun at the zoo?" Sal asked as he scooped Joey up in his arms.

"It was great!"

"I can't wait to hear all about it."

"I've got to finish up dinner. You boys enjoy yourselves." Vickie walked into the kitchen but paid attention to what Joey told Sal. She hoped he would remember not to mention Phil.

"Now, Marie, it's none of our business what goes on between them."

"How can you say that, Al, after what that woman has put them through? Now she's getting that sweet innocent child to lie for her."

Al placed his hand on her shoulder. He looked her in the eye with compassion. One of the things he loved about Marie was how much she cared about people. He knew Joey meant more to her than anyone else. That small child had somehow managed to attach himself to her heart in a way that nothing on earth could shake off. He also knew no good came from interference in other people's marriages. "I love you honey, but there is nothing we can do about this. He might get mad because you were spying on his wife. What if she finds out, and you're not allowed to see the boy anymore? It's none of our business."

Marie sighed. "I hate it when you make sense. It's very annoying." They laughed. "So we're supposed to just sit back and watch that woman hurt that good man *again*."

"You know, Marie, I couldn't stop you if you wanted to tell him. That's really up to you."

Marie looked at him. "You know what?"

"What?"

"I love you... even when you make me think something is my decision."

Rose grabbed her keys. She was running late for Bible study. She opened the door and screamed.

"Seriously Sis, way to make me feel welcomed."

"I wasn't expecting anyone at my door. I was on my way out."

"Really. That's too bad 'cause I happen to have your favorite DVD of all time in my purse and mint chocolate chip ice cream in this bag." She held the bag up for her to see.

"No brainer. Bible study will be there next week. Come in." She let Candice in and it dawned on her that she was probably there to spy on her. Her sister often received favors from their mom in exchange for information. "What did Ma tell you, Candy?"

"Wow, so suspicious. First you greet me with a scream and now you're accusing me of spying for Ma." She went into the kitchen and got two spoons for the ice cream. She plopped down on the couch. "Here's the DVD. Since you're so distrustful, *Arsenic and Old Lace* should go great with your mood."

Rose turned the television on and put the DVD in. "Give me one of those spoons."

"So, I hear you've been hanging out with Sal again."

"Yeah. You're not here on any mission from Ma. Go ahead and deny it now."

"Alright. She told me about Sal. I may be younger than you, but I still remember how that horrible man broke your heart."

"That was a long time ago. If we hadn't broken up, then I never would've met Duane,... and that would have been a... tragedy. He was the love of my life."

"Sorry, sis. I didn't mean to..."

"It's okay. I know you meant well. But I promise you that Sal and I are just friends. He's married and is going through a hard time with his wife. I'm grieving the loss of my husband." Candice placed a spoonful of ice cream in her mouth and gave her sister a look. "Seriously. There's nothing to worry about."

"Okay. If you say so."

"I do... hey, how did you get here anyway?"

"Ma loaned me her car."

"Snap. That woman is worried about me."

Candice sighed. "First of all, no one says, "snap" anymore. Secondly, she may have a point. Why set yourself up like this?"

"I'm not setting myself up for anything."

"Really. You're grieving the loss of your husband and the only other man that you ever loved is back in your life supporting you. Let's not forget the fact that his marriage has been a complete nightmare."

"How do you know?"

"I hear things."

"You mean, overhear."

"Whatever." Candice paused; she reached over to her sister and placed a loving hand on her shoulder. "I love ya and... I really want to watch this movie again... so what do ya say?"

Rose smiled. "Fine. I'll start it." While the opening credits played, Rose whispered, "I love you too, Candy."

"I know."

Nadine Zawacki

Chapter 10

The quiet in the apartment was deafening to Rose. It was time she faced the unopened boxes in the spare room. She felt frozen in time. The hallway to the spare room grew before her eyes. Her feet felt like bricks cemented to the ground, but she proceeded toward the door. She took a deep breath as her hand turned the doorknob. "Why does the air feel so thick in here?" she asked out loud to no one but herself. "Why won't my legs move? These are only boxes Rose. Get a grip... and it might help if you stop talking to yourself."

She stepped into the room slowly and approached the box closest to her. She cut open the tape with the box cutter in her hand. With caution she opened it up. Peanuts covered the top. "I have no idea what's in there. It must be fragile if I covered it up with all these peanuts. Again with the talking out loud." She reached in and pulled out a desk lamp. She uttered, "See... a lamp. I could use you on the desk in the bedroom." Rose shook her head as she opened up another box and then another. "Nothing scary in any of these boxes. I can do this." She was on a roll but wasn't prepared for what was inside the next one. She pulled out her wedding photo. She felt like she was punched in the gut. She went down on her knees. Held it in her hands. Tears flooded her face as she looked upon one of the happiest days in her life.

"Why Lord? So many hopes and dreams that were left unrealized... Why couldn't I have a child to... to... " Her tears soon turned into uncontrollable sobs. "Stop it, Rose! Just stop it. He's gone, and you have to move on." Her cell phone rang. It startled her. She tried to calm herself down before she reached for it. She breathed in deeply.

"Sal?... I'm not sure I'm up for coffee," she said between sobs. "No, I'm fine... really." The tears couldn't be contained. "It's just that... I was... emptying... boxes and... found my... wedding picture... No, you don't have to come over... okay... okay... I'll see you in a bit."

Sal came out of his office and was half way to the door when Margaret stopped him by shouting out, "Hey Sal, where's the fire?"

Sal turned around, "No fire. I'm going out to help a friend. I'll be back."

"A friend... I see... is this a flowery named friend?"

Sal chuckled, "Margaret, I know you're worried about my friendship with Rose, but really she's just going through a tough time."

Margaret just gave him that look of disapproval that Sal knew better to argue with. He loved Vickie and there was no concern in his mind that Rose was nothing more than just a friend. "I'll see you later," he uttered as he exited, not giving Margaret a chance to speak.

He was about to start his car when his cell rang. Sal let out a sigh—it was Vickie. "Hey, baby, what's up?... No, um I'm on way out of the store on... an errand and I can't come home for lunch... I'm sorry too, baby. I'll see you later. Give the little guy a kiss for me." *Now why did you lie to Vickie? It could be that she just wouldn't understand your friendship with Rose, or is it that you don't understand it?*

Sal arrived at Rose's apartment and rang the doorbell. She opened the door and he was surprised by her appearance. Her makeup ran down her face and her hair looked as if she had just gotten out of bed. The Rose he knew always dressed just so, even when they jogged together? It amazed him that she never sweated or managed to have a hair out of place while they jogged. He stepped in, reached out to her, and held her in his arms. She started to weep. His heart broke. "I'm sorry, Rose. Just let it out. I'm here. You don't have to face this alone."

It seemed like an eternity had passed when Rose finally stopped weeping. "I'm so sorry. I got your shirt all messed up."

"That's okay. It'll wash out."

"No, really... I have some stuff that will get that right out before it sets in." When Rose entered back into the room, she had a stain stick in her hand. "This works like magic, I promise." She dabbed it on his shirt. "There... it will dry up in no time."

"Thanks."

"I must look like a sight."

"You look fine. Are you okay?"

"I feel better now. It was good to let it out. I thought I was strong enough to go through our things. I just wasn't expecting my reaction to our wedding picture. We looked so happy... and when I saw his face... I just..." Tears filled her eyes. "I just started to remember all of our hopes... and dreams..." When she looked at Sal his heart melted. There were times when his marriage was horrendous and hurtful, but Vickie wasn't dead. She wasn't gone forever. There was hope. He instinctively reached out to her again and held her in his arms. This felt so right. For a moment he felt like nothing else mattered and no one else existed. She looked up at him, and he felt the urge to kiss her. It was stronger than an urge. It was desire. He stood there for a long time, but he moved back from their embrace. Sal knew this was a potentially dangerous situation. Awkward silence lingered.

"How rude of me. You've been here for a while, and I haven't offered you anything to drink."

"I'm fine. I don't need anything."

"No... really... let's see what I have." He followed her into the kitchen. She opened the refrigerator. "Hmmm... um... how about some milk?" She opened it up and smelled it. "Maybe not." They both laughed.

"Water would be fine, thanks."

Vickie didn't like the way Sal sounded on the phone. It was as if he was hiding something from her. She was an expert at lying and recognized it easily. After she dropped Joey off at the Delfeno's she headed for the candy store.

She entered the store from the back with her key. She looked into Sal's office and saw he wasn't there. "Hello, Margaret."

Margaret looked surprised. "Vickie dear, what are you doing here?"

"It's my store isn't it?"

"Of course. It's just you don't usually come in here without Joey. How is the lad doing?

"He's fine," she said curtly. "Where's Sal?"

"I believe he's out."

Hmmm. Interesting. Margaret didn't look her in the eyes. "Out where?"

"I don't rightly know."

"Really. That's your answer. You don't *rightly know.* I find that hard to believe Margaret. You always know more than you should."

"I'm not sure what you're getting at dear."

"Stop... calling... me... dear," she said through clenched teeth. "It's so irritating. Just tell me where he is?"

"Vickie as much as you think I know everything, I don't. He's your husband. Maybe you should put a leash on him."

She hated this woman for many reasons. Right now she had to curb the urge to punch her in the face. She didn't care if she was old. He must be with that woman, Rose. Why else would this old bat try to cover for him?

"Thanks for nothing. You're totally useless. I'll just call him." As she turned to leave she yelled, "Always a pleasure, Margaret."

Vickie got out to her car. She sat there steaming. He said he'd had coffee with her. Maybe that's where he is now. She'll just go to his favorite coffee shop and see for herself. It's hard to believe that she obsessed over his whereabouts. All the times she kept him guessing where she was, what she was doing and who she was with. It's true about payback, if that's what this was.

Sal sat in a chair while Rose sat on the couch. She had washed up. Even without make-up she was a stunner. They looked at each awkwardly. He kept fighting the desire to take her in his arms and kiss her. Rose broke the silence first.

"Thank you for making sure I didn't have a total nervous breakdown."

"That's what friends do, right."

"Right... friends. Sal, you and I both know that what we feel for each other is anything but *friendly*."

"I don't know what to say, Rose."

"Don't say anything. It's really important to keep in mind that emotions are flying high. I'm missing my husband and you're having some issues with your wife. That's all that this is. We can't fall back on the familiar. We didn't work the first time around for a reason. Maybe it would be best if we just cooled our *friendship* for awhile."

Sal looked down at his glass of water. He placed it on the coffee table. "I don't want to do that. I value your friendship. It's so easy to be around you."

"I guess if I can avoid crying like a baby and you can resist holding me, then we can do this friendship thing." They both chuckled.

"It's a deal." He felt as if something lifted from him. Something that didn't belong, and now clarity took its place. Sal got up and shook her hand. "I better get going. I don't want you to hesitate to call me if you need anything."

"Thanks Sal. You're a good man. Vickie is a blessed woman."

Sal hoped in his heart that Vickie thought so. He felt much better now about his friendship with Rose now that they had cleared the air. It frightened him how close he had come to betraying his vows. Whatever happened from this point forward, he felt confident that he would be true to the story he'd told—they are just friends. If that was a test, then he felt like he passed.

Chapter 11

Vickie waited for Sal to get home. She had gone to the coffee shop, but he wasn't there. She tried his cell, but it went straight to voice mail. She allowed her imagination to run rampant, which resulted in a frenzied state. The moment Sal walked into the door, she pounced on him like a leopard on a gazelle.

"Where were you today?"

"Work."

"I stopped by and you weren't there."

"I went on an errand, but I told you that when you called. Why did you stop by when you knew I wouldn't be there?"

Vickie tried to read Sal's facial expressions, but he was cautious. She decided a direct approach would catch him off guard. "Were you with that woman, Rose?" Sal's expression wasn't hard to miss. She got him. "Remember, Sally, I can read you like a book. If you lie to me, I'll know it."

"I got a call from Rose. She was distraught."

"So Sally had to ride in on his white horse and rescue the damsel in distress," she said mockingly.

Sal paused. "She just needed someone to talk to. She was going through some old boxes and found a wedding photo."

Compassion wasn't her strong suit, but this story sounded lame. "I don't care what set her off. I don't like the idea of you running to the rescue of another woman. It can lead to other things."

"And you would know," he fired back.

Vickie felt those words deep in her soul. All the trouble she caused—the drugs, the affairs. Right now that didn't matter to her. She might have hit a nerve to cause such a reaction. She stood there, speechless. It strengthened her resolve. She was not about to back down. One thing had nothing to do with another.

"I'm sorry, Vickie. That was a low blow."

"No need. I underestimated this woman. You have feelings for her, don't you, Sally?"

"The only feelings I have are feelings of compassion towards a friend's pain."

"Compassion... humph... that's a nice respectable word. "

"You're reading more into this than you should. *Nothing* is going on between us."

"Then why lie to me about where you're going or who you're with!"

"I... just... didn't tell you."

"Okay then, let me rephrase—don't 'leave out' information about your day or your whereabouts. Omission is worse than lying because you knew it would bother me, yet you did it anyway. I may not have gone to college, but I'm not stupid. I don't like it one bit!"

"And I don't like coming home and finding you face down in your own vomit!" She didn't have a comeback for that. She watched as he took a deep breath and walked over to her. She felt as if she couldn't breathe. She wanted to slap him, but instead his words paralyzed her. She wanted to melt away. What she wouldn't do for a hit right now. Sal stood in front of her. He looked deeply in her eyes. "I love you and only you. I promised to love you and cherish you in sickness and in health. In good times and in bad, forsaking all others. I'm a man of my word. I couldn't hurt you that way."

"As opposed to me."

"Listen... I love you, period."

Vickie bit her lip, as was her custom when she felt frustrated. She had no idea what to say or do at this point. She just needed a break. She needed time to think. Vickie knew her personality flaws. Sal's good character made her feel inferior about herself. "I need a cigarette. I don't have any."

"I'll go to the store for you."

"It's okay. I know you don't like it when I smoke, so you don't have to go. I can go to the store myself. It'll give me a chance to clear my head. Joey's downstairs with the Delfenos."

"Okay. I'll go get him. How about pizza for dinner?"

"Sure. Fine. Whatever. I'll be back." Vickie grabbed her purse and slammed the door on her way out.

Henry and Ida went for walk. As much as they enjoyed the Nelsons' company, they cherished their alone time. They weren't used to being surrounded by people everyday. The street was lined with beautiful, well-kept homes. The gardens in front of these homes were some of the most beautiful Henry had ever seen. The variety of flowers, bushes and trees was endless. The colors exploded. Henry loved colors for they reminded him of God. God must love color, why else would He have created the world as He did? At the end of the street was a small community park. A slide and monkey bars were located in the center of the park. Benches lined the play area, so parents could watch their children. Henry and Ida sat down on one of the benches to rest. "So Ida, are you enjoying our time in New York?"

"More than I expected to Henry. How long do you suppose we'll be here?"

"I don't rightly know. I sensed that something bad is about to happen. I've been praying for God's mercy."

"I'm sure the Lord will protect those involved."

Henry smiled. Ida had a simple faith that always seemed to trust God. Even when she had miscarried two of their children her faith had never wavered. It's more than Henry could say for himself. He was grateful for the three sons the Lord did bless them with, Henry, Jonah and Isaac. Isaac's son, Connor, seemed to operate on the same level of prophetic gifting as his grandfather. From the time he was a little boy he saw angels. He often called grandpa when he had experiences he couldn't explain. He'd graduate with a teaching degree in a year. He couldn't be prouder of him.

"There's a church I need to go visit, Ida. I need to visit it alone if that's okay with you."

"Oh, Henry, you worry too much. My feelings aren't hurt. I understand the life God has called you to. You go spend time with Him. Take as long as you need. It's what makes you the man that you are."

Henry smiled. "Ida, that's why I love you—madly and passionately."

"Oh Henry, you behave now."

"It's hard to behave around you darling."

"I'm an old woman, Henry James. You remember that."

"You're my old woman Ida—you remember that!" Ida smiled in such a way that her eyes twinkled, or at least they did to Henry.

"Let's head on back. We don't want to worry our guests, now do we?"

"Okay. You win—this time," he smiled as he kissed her hand.

"Henry James, you ole charmer."

Chapter 12

Vickie walked right into Phil as she left the bodega. "Are you following me?"

"Guilty as charged," Phil replied with his hand held up in surrender. "I'm worried about you, baby. I don't trust that goody goody you're married to. No one is that honest."

Her anger at Sal made running into Phil a dangerous situation. Sal made her feel bad about herself. Phil just accepted her as she was. She placed a cigarette to her lips and Phil offered her a light.

"What's the matter babe? You look upset."

"I just had a fight with Sal."

"Tell me about it. It'll be good for you to get it off your beautiful chest."

"He's been getting friendly with an ex, Rose something or another, then lying to me about it."

"Really now... Mr. Faithful has been lying about another woman?"

Vickie was sorry she'd mentioned it. "Forget it. If you're only going to be a punk, then why should I bother talking to you?"

"I'm sorry. Don't be mad. I can be serious."

Vickie looked into his eyes. He changed his expression. "Well, it's the woman he use to date before me. She called him today, and he went running to her side. Something about her being upset over her dead husband. He even went out to coffee with her the other day, and if it wasn't for the fact that I caught him in a lie, he wouldn't have told me about it." She watched his expression, but noticed that he seemed to be listening without his usual mocking eyes, so she continued. "I have every right to be mad, don't I?"

"Are you asking me?" he sounded sincere.

"Yeah... I mean, it sounds fishy doesn't it?"

"Well, if it was as innocent as he claims, then he wouldn't lie about it. People only lie when they are doing something wrong."

"Well he said he didn't lie... he just didn't tell me."

"Ah... well omission is just like lying, especially if you're just being a wuss trying to save your own skin."

"Yeah! My point exactly."

"If I were you, I would demand he not see her again. You're his wife, and you have every right to approve of his friends."

"You're right. He's my husband not hers."

"I think she's trying to replace her dead husband with your live one."

Phil was making sense to her. It's exactly what she was thinking. "Thanks, Phil. You're right. I'll talk to you later."

"I've got your back, babe."

Sal knocked on the Delfenos' door. Marie answered, "Hello, Sal. I bet you're here for Joey. He's asleep on the couch. He was so tired. I hope it's okay."

Sal walked in as he said, "That's fine. Thank you for watching him."

"It's always a pleasure. I... never mind."

Sal noticed a worried look on her face. "Is something wrong Mrs. Delfeno?"

"Well it's probably none of my business, but I just wouldn't feel right about keeping this from you."

He wasn't sure if he wanted to know, but asked anyway, "Keeping what from me?"

"I overheard something that concerned me."

Sal wanted nothing to do with gossip. "Well then maybe you shouldn't say anything. You could have overheard incorrectly."

"I heard very clearly."

Sal sighed. "I don't want to hear stories about other people."

"It's not about other people. It concerns you."

Curiosity got the best of him. "Me?"

"I'm afraid so. I thought about not telling you, but it involves Joey."

When it came to Joey, Sal had a hard time keeping his composure. "Then say it!... I'm sorry, I didn't mean to snap at you."

"It's okay. This isn't easy for me either. I heard Vickie tell Joey to lie to you about 'her friend' that bought him ice cream at the zoo."

Sal's breathing labored. He looked at Mrs. Delfeno and asked, "What friend?"

"She didn't say. She just told Joey that it was a secret from you. Something about she didn't want you to feel badly about not being at the zoo to buy Joey ice cream."

"I see... Don't worry about that Mrs. Delfeno, Vickie already told me about it."

"Oh good. Al told me I should keep out of it, but I thought you should know."

"Yeah, it's fine. Thanks for watching Joey."

"Anytime."

Vickie felt empowered by her conversation with Phil. She was going to give Sal a piece of her mind and demand he stop helping that witch. She walked in to find Sal sitting on the couch. "Where's Joey?"

"He's asleep in his room."

"Good, because we need to talk."

Sal got up slowly, and she didn't like the look in his eyes. "Yeah we do. Let's start with who bought Joey ice cream at the zoo?"

Vickie was taken aback by his question. *How did he know?* "Oh, that... did Joey say something?"

"No. I'm not playing that game with you. Who was it? It was Phil wasn't it?" Vickie reached for a cigarette. "Don't light that in here," he said curtly.

"Sorry. I... I don't know what to say."

"How about the truth for once."

"Yeah. It was Phil, but I didn't invite him. He just showed up and bought us ice cream. And the reason I didn't say anything was because I knew it would upset you."

"I thought you promised never to see him again."

"I told you he just showed up. What do you think a five year old would say to someone offering to buy him ice cream?" She felt defensive.

Sal pursed his lip. She saw him do that only when he was mad. "You lied, or should I say *omitted* the truth. You got mad at me for doing the same thing, except I never cheated on you with Rose."

She didn't like that he threw that in her face. He was right, but she wasn't going to let him win. "Hey one thing doesn't have anything to do with the other. You may not have cheated, but tell me you weren't tempted."

A tear fell down Sal's face. "I'm at a loss, Vickie. Why don't you love me?"

Vickie shook her head. He was so whiny sometimes. She hated it when he got this way. "I do love you. I'm sorry I hurt you," she said in a tone a child would say just to get her parent to back off. *How many times do I have to apologize?*

Sal got up and came toward her. He placed his hands on her upper arms and then pulled her close. He held her tightly in his arms.

Great. Now he's touching me. She just wanted him to stop. He can be such a touchy feely kind of guy that it made her want to puke. She had more respect for him when he got mad. At least then he showed emotion she could respect. Phil wouldn't act that way. "Let's not hurt each other anymore. I'll stay away from Rose if you'll stay away from Phil. Is that a deal?"

She placed her arms around his waist and replied, "It's a deal." She knew what she had to do at that moment. She just couldn't live like this anymore. She just wanted to be free from this prison called marriage.

Sal had trouble sleeping that night. He felt as if Vickie was holding something back from him. He decided it would be best if he went to church and just spend some time praying. Maybe he could find answers there. Vickie was still asleep. He didn't want to wake her. He checked on Joey and found him sleeping soundly in his bed. It was too early to wake him. It was a good time to slip away. The church would be quiet.

He loved that Father Robert left the doors opened all the time. It did cause problems sometimes, but Father Robert wanted the community to have a place they could come to be with God. He entered and found that there was an old man in the last pew. He looked up when Sal walked in and nodded in his direction. Sal nodded in return.

Sal walked up to the front of the church and sat down. He sat there quietly and started to pray. He wept silently. He felt his head spin and he wasn't sure if he stood up he would faint. He prayed for Vickie. *If only my Dad were still alive, he would know what to do.*

Henry sat in the back of the church. He could sense the turmoil in Sal's heart. He prayed for guidance. He wasn't told to approach him. So he continued to watch from the back. Sal got up and Henry noticed the sadness in his face. He wanted to ease his pain, so he quietly prayed for him and his family.

Chapter 13

After he left the church, Sal found himself at the cemetery. He knelt down by his father's grave.

Joseph Michael Martinelli
Husband—Father—Friend

His father's life summed up in three words. His mind drifted to when he first met Vickie. She was beautiful even though she looked like a wet cat as she sat on that park bench in the rain...

"Are you okay?" Sal asked. She sniffed as she nodded. Sal had recently ended his relationship with Rose. He had a change of heart and was on his way back to her dorm room to make up with her when he spotted a girl crying on a bench in the rain. She looked so despondent. He felt drawn to her. It was as if he had no control of his movements. He walked over to cover her with his umbrella. "Hi... my name is Sal."

"So."

"I don't mean to intrude..."

Her mascara trailed down her cheeks, yet she was still stunning. Her eyes captivated him. They pulled on his heartstrings. "Sorry... it's just... I've got... no... place..."

He finished her sentence for her "to go."

"Yeah."

He wasn't sure why but, he extended his hand. "Come with me. I live about a block away. You can get warm and out of those wet clothes."

Wide eyed she looked at him. "Look Mister I'm not that type of girl. I may be alone, wet and desperate but

I'm not going to sleep with you just to get out of the rain."

"No... no... that's not what I meant. I can loan you some clothes—granted they would be men's clothes—to change into until your clothes dry. All I'm offering is a warm cup of tea." She smiled.

"Are you messing with me?" Sal asked when he saw her smile.

"Yeah, Boy Scout, I am... Sorry, old habit. I guess I could use some hot tea and dry clothes."

Before he knew it, they were back at his apartment. Sal made her some tea while she took off her wet clothes. He wasn't sure why he was doing this for a stranger he just met. She looked morose. His friends always teased him about being a sucker for tears. He walked into the living room with a cup of tea in his hands to find her on the couch wearing his blue shirt and nothing else from what he could see. He nearly dropped the cup.

"Those clothes you gave me were too big. I hope you don't mind I borrowed this shirt instead."

"No... um... here's your tea."

"Thanks, Boy Scout."

"Just call me Sal." He cleared his throat. "You never told me your name."

"I know," she said as she took a sip of tea.

Not knowing what else to say, Sal continued. "You want to talk about why you were sitting out in the rain crying?" *What a stupid thing to say. She won't give you her name... why would she tell you anything else?*

She placed her teacup on the coffee table and looked right at him. "I'm homeless. My boy... ex just threw me out. We got into a big fight. He didn't even let me take any of my stuff. I've got no family and no place to go. Is that what you wanted to hear, Boy Scout?"

"Hey, I just met you. You looked miserable sitting there in the rain. I'm just trying to help."

She got up. "No one asked you to!"

He walked over to her. He placed his hand on her shoulder. He wasn't convinced of her tough exterior. "I wasn't trying to insult you. I'm sorry if I did."

"You *are* a boy scout aren't you? I bet you take in all kinds of strays." Sal started to wonder why he was trying to help this difficult woman.

"You're free to go anytime, but your clothes aren't dry yet. Please... sit. We don't have to talk."

She sat back down on the couch, and Sal sat in the chair. He didn't speak again. He saw a tear go down her cheek, but resisted the urge to say anything. Finally she broke the silence. "Vickie."

"I beg your pardon."

"My name. It's Vickie." She smiled. The dryer buzzed and startled both of them.

"It's only the dryer. Your clothes are probably dry. Let me check. I'll be right back."

Sal heard the doorbell. He overheard Vickie talk to someone as he reentered the room. "Hi. Can I help you?"

Sal came to the door. "Rose. What are you doing here?"

"It was a mistake to come here." She started to leave.

He realized what it must look like to Rose the way Vickie was dressed. "Oh no. This is not what it looks like Rose. I can explain."

"No need. I came here to tell you that you were right to break things off. The truth of the matter is I've moved on. I know how guilty you get about things and just wanted to let you off the hook."

"Boy Scout, right."

"Vickie, please go inside." She turned and walked back to the couch. He lowered his voice. "I barely know her. It's a long story, but nothing happened here. It was raining..."

"Sal. Stop. No more. It's over." Rose walked away.

Sal knew Rose well enough to know she needed to calm down. She wouldn't listen to him in her state of mind. Who could blame her? She came here to find another woman dressed in his shirt.

"Sorry. Didn't mean to get you in trouble."

"I'm not in trouble. She's my... my ex." Sal walked over and sat next to Vickie on the couch. She placed her hand on his leg.

"Now you look sad, Boy Scout."

"Could you just call me Sal?" he said exasperated.

"Sorry... Sal. You've been so kind. No one has ever treated me this way." She stroked his leg with her hand. He hated to admit how good the feel of her hand felt against his leg. He knew he should remove it, but... "Look Sal. You've done so much already. I even hate to ask this but... I was wondering if it would be okay for me to spend the night on your couch?" She inched her way closer to him. Her sad eyes weren't sad at the moment. He could hear her breathing start to labor. He felt his pulse speed up. He wasn't sure what happened. At first she had seemed to hate him, but now...

He swallowed. "Sure. No problem."

"Thank you." She inched closer to his face. "Do you mind if I sleep in your shirt?" Their lips were so close now he could taste her.

"No. I don't mind." With that she kissed him and he let her. He was surprised by the tenderness of her kiss. Goosebumps went down his leg. He stood up and she stood with him. Their lips never parted. It was one of the most passionate kisses he'd ever had. Without giving Rose a second thought, he picked her up and headed to the bedroom.

Sal smiled at the happy memory. "Oh Pops, what am I going to do? I wish you were here. You were always so full of wisdom. I'm confused. I don't know what I was thinking. What if I had just run after Rose that day? What would my life be like today? I guess it doesn't matter. I broke up with Rose for a reason. We were always better as friends. I have Joey. I can't imagine life without him. He's such a good boy, Pops. He has a lot of you in him." Sal got up and brushed the dirt from his pants. A sudden chill ran through him. He knew it was time to go home, but it was the last place he wanted to be.

Nadine Zawacki

Chapter 14

Vickie leaned against the kitchen counter. She gazed at Joey as he drew pictures. He looked up at her. A smile formed on her face. He was the closest thing to love she ever felt. Her mind wandered off to the first time she met Sal. He was such a Boy Scout. It was raining....

Vickie wasn't sure how long she sat there on that bench in the rain. Her umbrella broke, which was the last straw. She was soaked to the bone. She just gave up, and all she could do was cry. In the mist of her breakdown Vickie heard someone ask, "Are you okay?" She sniffed and nodded. She didn't know what to say. He came closer and covered her with his umbrella. He stood there and introduced himself, "Hi... my name is Sal."

"So."

"I don't mean to intrude..."

She looked a mess between the rain and the tears. Could this be a knight in shining armor about to come to her rescue? She wasn't sure if she could respond, but managed "Sorry... it's just... I've got... no... place..."

She couldn't utter another word when he did it for her, "to go."

"Yeah."

"Come with me. I live about a block away. You can get warm and out of those wet clothes."

This could work out to her advantage, but she needed to play her cards close to the vest. Kindness brought out her sarcastic side. It could be because she never met anyone who didn't want something in return. "Look Mister I'm not that type of girl. I may be alone, wet and desperate but I'm not going to sleep with you just get out of the rain." *Or maybe I will. This Boy Scout is really cute.* His awkward response made her feel better...

"No... no... that's not what I meant. I can loan you some clothes—granted they would be men's clothes—to change into until your clothes dry. All I'm offering is a warm cup of tea..." She smiled.... "Are you messing with me?" he asked when she smiled at him.

Of course she was. There was something about this guy that was different from the usual low life characters she was attracted to. She attributed her bad taste in men from being bounced around from one foster home to another. Somehow foster mothers blamed her when their husband forced themselves on her. *Stop it Vickie. No excuses. You are who you are—a survivor.*

"Yeah, Boy Scout, I am... Sorry, old habit. I guess I could use some hot tea and dry clothes."

All the way to his apartment she thought how the universe had looked out for her. *Desperate times....* She might be able to wiggle into his world and have a place to stay. That would irritate Phil so much that he would take her back. Nothing made a man want you more than when he couldn't have you.

He left her in his room to change. She looked at the pants, boxers and T-shirt he left on the bed for her to change into. *Those are not going to do for what I have in mind.* She looked around the room. He lived very simply. The furniture was modern with clean lines. She noticed all the books on his desk. *Hmmm... he must be a student... smart I bet.* She opened the closet door and found a button-down shirt that would work nicely for what she had in store. She went out to the living room and sat on the couch. *Here comes the Boy Scout now with some tea. How sweet. This will be easier than I thought.*

She thought his eyes would fall out of his head when he looked at her. "Those clothes you gave me were too big. I hope you don't mind, I borrowed this instead."

"No... um... here's your tea."

He really is shy. I'm not sure if it's cute or pathetic. "Thanks, Boy Scout."

"Just call me Sal." He cleared his throat. "You never told me your name."

"I know." *It's not going to be that easy pal.* She sipped her tea.

"You want to talk about why you were sitting out in the rain crying?" *Thanks for the opening.*

She placed her tea on the table. "I'm homeless. My boy... ex just threw me out. We got into a big fight." *Now for the rest of the sob story...* "He didn't even let me take any of my stuff. I've got no family and no place to go. Is that what you wanted to hear, Boy Scout?"

"Hey, I just met you. You looked miserable sitting there in the rain. I'm just trying to help."

That's right Vickie work it... a little pride would do about now.... She got up. "No one asked you to!"

When he got up and placed his hand on her shoulder, she knew she had him. "I wasn't trying to insult you. I'm sorry if I did."

"You *are* a boy scout aren't you? I bet you take in all kinds of strays."

"You're free to go anytime, but your clothes aren't dry yet. Please... sit. We don't have to talk."

Nadine Zawacki

Oh no, too far. What I need now is to rope him back in, but how? Ah... this always works on boy scouts. A tear ran down her cheek, and she broke the silence with "Vickie."

"I beg your pardon."

"My name. It's Vickie." Something buzzed really loud and startled her.

"It's only the dryer. Your clothes are probably dry. Let me check. I'll be right back."

Vickie heard the doorbell. She instinctively got up, peeked through the peephole and noticed a pretty woman. She smiled to herself and opened the door. "Hi. Can I help you?" *Hmmm... good she's leaving.*

Suddenly Sal was right behind her. "Rose. What are you doing here?"

"It was a mistake to come here."

Sal looked at her, and she tried to look as innocent as she could. "Oh no. This is not what it looks like, Rose. I can explain."

"No need. I came here to tell you that you were right to break things off. The truth of the matter is I've moved on. I know how guilty you get about things and just wanted to let you off the hook."

Vickie interjected, "Boy Scout, right."

"Vickie, please go inside." *Damage done.*

She went inside and sat back on the couch. She could hear them, but it was hushed. When he closed the door, she figured it didn't go well. "Sorry. Didn't mean to get you into trouble."

"I'm not in trouble. She's my... my ex." To her surprise he sat next to her. Never one to let an opportunity go by, she placed her hand on his leg.

88

"Now you look sad, Boy Scout."

"Could you just call me Sal?"

"Sorry... Sal." She stroked his leg with her hand. He didn't protest so she continued, "Look Sal. You've done so much already... I even hate to ask this but... " *Easy now Vickie. Don't spook him.* "I was wondering if it would be okay for me to spend the night on your couch?" She moved in closer to him. She batted her eyes ever so subtly. His breathing labored. She could feel electricity build between.

"Sure. No problem." *Hook.*

She was close enough to kiss him, but didn't. She wanted him to come closer to her. "Thank you." *Line.* She inched closer to his face. "Do you mind if I sleep in your shirt?" She could almost taste his lips. She knew he was hungry now.

"No. I don't mind." With that she kissed him softly at first and then with increased passion. She stood up with him, their lips never parted. He picked her up and headed to the bedroom. *Sinker.*

"Mommy... Mommy..." she heard Joey's voice and it was back to reality.

"What is it baby?"

"I made you a picture. Do you like it?"

"It's beau... I mean a very handsome picture." He smiled up at her. "So what is it?"

"It's our family. Daddy... you... and me," he said with pride.

She looked at her son and felt guilt wash over her. Sal was an honorable man, and she's been hateful. "Well, let's hang it up so Daddy can see it when he comes home."

Nadine Zawacki

Chapter 15

"Look Candy, I know you mean well but... okay... Tell Mom that I'll go to the meeting... Yes, of course I promise... No, I'm not mad... This is my exasperated voice, not my mad one... Yeah, yeah, love you too." Rose hung up. She knew they meant well, but now she was stuck going to a bereavement group meeting at church. It was the last place she wanted to go, but she had promised. She might as well get it over with. Somehow she knew her mom would find out if she bailed. She grabbed her keys and headed out the door.

As she was about to get into her car, she turned around suddenly. She didn't see anything out of the ordinary—people going about their business. She had an inexplicable feeling that she was being watched. *First you talk to yourself and now you're letting your imagination go wild.* She got into her car and drove toward the church. She had enough time to stop for a caffeine fix. She needed the boost if she had to face a group of strangers. She wanted to move on, not look back. These meetings tended to be too emotional for her taste. What was the point in rehashing pain?

Sal walked into the apartment. "I'm home." He heard Joey and Vickie in the kitchen. As he entered, Vickie smiled. It was a welcomed change from her usual tense gaze. Maybe things have improved.

"Daddy!" Joey yelled as he jumped into Sal's arms.

"Hey, Buddy. I missed you today."

"I missed you too, Daddy."

"Go wash up, Bud. Dinner will be ready soon." Vickie interjected.

"Okay, Mommy."

When he left, Sal observed that her eyes were sad. "Are you okay?"

"Yeah." She turned around.

"You don't look okay." He gently turned her facing toward him. "I love you. You can tell me anything." He found it difficult to reach her at times.

"I know." She kissed him gently on the lips. "You should wash up too. Dinner will be ready in about ten minutes."

"Okay." What else could he do? He wished he knew how to soften her heart toward him. As he washed his hands, his mind drifted off to Rose. He had loved her once, or was it just a college thing?

"Dinner's ready." He was grateful that his thoughts were interrupted by Vickie's voice. Thoughts of Rose lead to complications he didn't need.

"Coming." He had to concentrate on the present and leave the past where it belonged—in the past. He walked into the kitchen. Joey and Vickie were already seated. He joined them. Pride rose up within him when he looked at Joey. He loved that boy so much. Whenever he doubted his relationship with Vickie, he was reminded of the good that came out of it—Joey. His cell phone rang. Vickie watched him closely.

"Aren't you going to answer it?"

"Nope. I'm having dinner with my family," he smiled contently.

Rose decided not to leave a message for Sal. She wasn't sure why she had called him anyway. She arrived at the church, but couldn't get out of the car. She thought a pep talk would help, hence the call to Sal. "Suck it up Rose. You promised you would go; just do it!" She took a deep breath. She watched as people entered the building. Rose was amazed by how many people had lost someone they loved. She got out of the car.

The room was packed. A podium peeked out in the front of the room. In the back corner was a small card table that offered coffee and cookies. She found a seat in the last row. The chairs filled up quickly as an attractive blonde-haired woman in her forties, Rose ventured a guess, stood behind the podium.

"My name is Anna Rogers. I see some new faces tonight. Welcome. I want to reassure you that whatever is said in here, stays in here. You can think of it as *Vegas*." The crowd chuckled at her joke. "This is a safe place. No one has to share if they don't want to. There is no pressure. We are all here because we have lost someone we loved. Sometimes it helps to know we aren't alone... that others understand our grief... our pain. So with that being said, would anyone like to go first?"

There was silence. Rose looked around. The last thing she wanted to do was to share her feelings. A slightly disheveled, but attractive man stood up.

"I'll share." He walked up to the front. Anna patted him on his shoulder. He cleared his throat. "Hello."

"Hello," everyone replied on cue.

"My name is Jeremy Harris. I came tonight because I made a promise to a friend to start to deal with my feelings... I lost my wife... 'lost.' That's such a funny term." He looked downward. Rose could see that he had trouble expressing himself. "I didn't misplace her... she was sick and then she died." He bought his fist up to his mouth. He looked around the room as if he could draw strength from it. "It was a tumor in her brain... she was intelligent, beautiful and kind... a combination that's not easy to come by..." His voice started to quiver. "We had no warning. It happened so fast. She was gone in an instant." A tear rolled down his face. A lump grew in Rose's throat. She was moved by his willingness to open up in front of a group of strangers. He was so... brave. "It's been about a year... yet... it still stings... everything reminds me of her. Everyone... well meaning friends and family... they want me to move on... I mean, what does that even mean?... I'm mad. I feel cheated. I'm the one who's lost. I'm lost without her... we'll never have... children... I mean why would I bother now... it wouldn't be the same without her... plans for a future... gone... I... I can't continue." Anna came up next to him.

"You did great Jeremy. You are not alone in this. So many of us feel the same way. Thank you for sharing and putting words to your emotions." Rose made unintentional eye contact with Jeremy. He smiled at her. It made her feel self-conscious; especially when she realized her eyes were filled with tears.

When the meeting ended, Rose felt better. She hated the fact that her mother was right, which meant she was wrong. It *did* help to hear others who shared a similar experience. It made her feel less alone. She got up to leave as soon as it was over. Rose didn't have it in her to talk to anyone. As she reached her car she heard, "Leaving so soon?" She turned around to find Jeremy standing there.

"I... um... it was my first time and... I guess I'm shy."

"Forgive me, I wasn't trying to make you feel bad. It's just... it was my first time here, too."

"I think you're brave for sharing like that." Rose felt like she was in high school again, not sure how to talk to a guy she just met.

"Sometimes I like to get the hard part over with, you know just be the first one to share. Then I can just sit back and listen." He smiled. It disarmed Rose. He was quite attractive, especially in the moonlight. "Hey... um... would you like to go for some coffee? We can talk or not talk?"

"Thanks, but I think I'm just going to head home." She felt awkward being asked out at such a meeting.

"I didn't mean it that way... I... I don't know why I asked really."

"That's okay. It's fine."

"I mean when I was standing up there, I saw you in the back.

You had a kind face and... never mind."

"Maybe next time I'll take you up on that coffee, but I really have to get home."

Jeremy's grin reminded her of that first time Duane asked her out. "I'm making an idiot out of myself. I stand up there and say how much I miss my wife and then ask you out for coffee. You must think I'm a hypocrite."

"No. I just was caught off guard."

"Sorry. I thought you looked like someone who would understand and we could talk... well, maybe next time."

"Yeah maybe next time. Good-night."

"Good-night."

Rose got into her car and was about to drive off when her phone rang. It was Sal. "Hello... yeah, I'm fine. I called because I was heading into a bereavement group at my church and I... um... was going to chicken out. I needed someone to talk me into it... No problem... I ended up talking myself into it... It was okay... It was a good thing I went... There was this guy who lost his wife and what he shared was so beautiful... I could totally relate... Sure, I'd love to have coffee tomorrow... See you then."

She smiled at the thought of seeing Sal again. *Maybe that's not a good thing. Ah, Rose, it's only coffee at a neutral place... then why, when he calls you, can't you stop smiling and your heart jumps up and down with excitement?... Yeah, right—just friends.*

Nadine Zawacki

Chapter 16

Sal ate his ham and eggs in silence. He was preoccupied with thoughts of Rose. All he could think about was his coffee date with her today. *Date?* That wasn't a good term... meeting is a better word. It was definitely more accurate. He looked forward to it more than he would admit to himself.

"What are you smiling about?" Vicki's question interrupted his reflections.

He felt as if she gave him the third degree whenever she asked questions of him. "Nothing really. I'm just happy."

Vickie glared at him suspiciously. "So... what do you have planned for today?"

"Nothing really. Just the same old same old." He took another bite of his eggs. He had a hard time looking Vicki in the eyes. He just didn't want to get into a fight over nothing. She doesn't understand that his relationship with Rose is simply friendship. Why get into another fight? "What about you?"

"Just taking Joey to school, cleaning... cooking. You know the same old same old." The sarcasm didn't escape, Sal.

"Look at the time. I better get going." Sal gave Joey a kiss on the head. "Have fun in school son."

"I always have fun."

Sal loved the lens of innocence through which Joey viewed life. There were days he would love to switch places with his son. As Vickie walked over to the table, he reached out to her. He felt her body stiffen at his touch. A piece of his heart died every time she did that. Undaunted, he kissed her on the cheek. "Enjoy your day, Baby. I'll see you later." She said nothing in return.

He reached his car, opened the door and sat there. He started the car. The radio was already on an oldie station. Elton John's song "Sorry Seems To Be The Hardest Word" was being played. No matter what he did he couldn't get Vickie to be consistent in her love for him.

The words to the song pulled on his emotions in a way he hadn't expected. He couldn't move. The tears flowed freely. He loved her with his whole heart, but she rarely returned his love. Was she even capable of it?

Rose arrived at the coffee house early. She waited anxiously for Sal when her phone rang. "Hi Mom... Of course I went. I promised didn't I?... Hey that's not fair; I keep my promises... Yes, it was fine... I'm not sure if I'll go again... because... Ma..." She spotted Sal. "Look, I gotta go... I promise I'll call you later when I have time... Ma, *please*... I love you too... okay, bye." She knew her mother loved her, but she suffocated her at times. Her smile was returned by Sal. He stood by the counter. She lifted her cup to show him she already had coffee. After his order was ready, he walked over to the table.

"Hey, how are you doing?" Sal asked.

"I'm fine. It's nice of you to take time to have coffee with me today."

"What are friends for? So how did your meeting go last night?"

"It was fine. It wasn't as bad as I thought it would be."

"Did you make any new friends?" he smirked. "Was he cute?"

"You're so funny." She rolled her eyes. "As a matter of fact. There was this guy there. He shared his story. It was like he was inside my head. He articulated what was on my own heart."

"A guy?" he smirked again.

"Don't be a child. He was a guy who was grieving the loss of his wife."

"So did this 'grieving guy' ask you out?"

Rose stammered, "Um... I... what?"

"That sounds like a yes."

"How did you know?" she asked stunned.

"Well, it's quite simple, my dear Watson. I'm a guy. I know how guys think. He saw this beautiful woman with what I'm assuming were sympathetic eyes, and he couldn't help himself."

Rose slapped him on the arm. He feigned being hurt. Her heart leaped a little when he called her a beautiful woman. Her mind drifted when suddenly she heard Sal's voice.

"Earth to Rose. Are you listening to me?"

"I'm sorry. Yes, I am. I had a conversation with my mom before you got here, and she's still stuck in my head."

"That's okay. What I asked was, did you say yes?"

"Yes to what?"

"To the date."

"Oh. It was more like he asked me for coffee, but it didn't happen."

"Well... I think you should."

His response surprised her. "Really?"

"Yeah... I mean you're free, and it would be good for you to start dating."

"Now you sound like my mother."

"Oops. Apologies. I didn't mean to step on your toes."

"No... it's not you... it's my mom... she sorta got under my skin before and I guess... it doesn't matter... everyone wants me to move on... I'm sorry." The silence between them felt uncomfortable. She didn't like that he too told her to move on.

"Rose, don't be upset."

"Who's upset?"

"Never mind. So what happened last night when you tried to call me?"

"I sat outside the meeting place. I guess I was having a bit of a panic attack."

"I'm so sorry I didn't pick up the phone," he smiled. His eyes sparkled whenever he smiled, or at least it seemed that way.

"I got over it. It was a good thing that I went in."

"Because of *Grieving Guy*."

Her cell phone rang. *Thank God.* "Excuse me. I should get this." She didn't recognize the number, but welcomed the interruption. "Hello... Oh, hi... How did you get my number?... Well, you're quite resourceful. " A girlish grin crossed her face as she tilted her head. "I don't know," she said and looked at Sal's face. "Okay... That sounds nice. How about I meet you there... Yes, seven o'clock sounds great."

Sal smiled at her, "Got a date?"

Rose chuckled. "Well yes. His name is Jeremy by the way, not *Grieving Guy*. He went to great lengths to get my number." She realized she had just put on a show for Sal. *What's wrong with you?*

"I'm sure he did," he smirked.

"Don't get smug. So I took your advice. We're going to have dinner tonight."

She thought Sal hesitated before he spoke. "That's good. I hope you have a good time."

"Thanks." Suddenly the mood changed. The silence was deafening. She checked her watch. "Wow, look at the time. I gotta go. I promised my mom I would stop by her house."

Sal stood up. "It's always nice seeing you, Rose."

"You too, Sal." They shared an awkward hug.

"Hey, let me know how your date goes tonight. I hope you have a nice time."

"Thanks." Since everyone wanted her to move forward, Jeremy was a good place to start.

Sal sat in his car for a moment. He wasn't sure how he felt about Rose and this Jeremy guy. He hoped that he was a good man. He would hate to see her get hurt. "Who are you kidding? You're jealous. Why? You're married, and she's not. It's good to remember that." He shook his head. It was time he went to the store.

When he reached the store, he took a deep breath. Margaret had a knack of knowing when something was wrong. He wasn't in the mood to talk about Vickie or Rose.

"Good morning, Margaret."

"Good afternoon is more like it, Boss."

"Stop it with the boss already, Margaret. It's not funny."

"Don't blame me if you don't have a sense a humor."

He laughed. "Anything happened that I should know about?"

"Your wife stopped by again. She's making a habit of it."

"Vickie?"

"Of course, Vickie. Do you have another wife I don't know about?"

"Did she say what she wanted?"

"She's your wife." Sal gave her look. "She commanded me not to tell you she came here."

"Margaret."

"Well maybe I stretched the truth a bit, but she said she'd rather I not mention her visit."

"I see." Sal wondered what Vickie was up to. She asked him what he was doing today and he lied. Now Vickie knows he lied.

"So... do you want to discuss it or not?"

"Margaret... seriously, it creeps me out when you do that."

Nadine Zawacki

Chapter 17

Vickie found herself at Marine Park. It was a comfort, her safe haven, a place she could retreat to find peace of mind. Sometimes she liked walking along the path, other times just sitting on a bench. Her chin rested on her legs as she sat on the bench. She was not sure how long she had been there, but she became more despondent as time passed. All she could think about was that woman and Sal. He was probably with her right now. It would serve her right if Sal finally left her once and for all. How long was a man expected to be faithful to a faithless wife? Her paranoia had no bounds. She realized at the moment there wasn't anything she wouldn't do for a hit.

"Hello, Sunshine." Came a familiar voice.

Startled, Vickie responded, "Phil! Seriously. Are you stalking me?"

"Who stole your candy, little girl?" She just rolled her eyes. "Hey, I'm just playing. What's wrong?"

"Bad day."

"How can old Phil help make it better?"

Don't do it Vickie. You're stronger than this. "I could use something to cheer me up?"

Phil looked at her with glee-filled eyes. He patted his jacket pocket. "I got a little something, if you really want it. Just say the word."

She bit her lower lip; her mind raced. Thoughts of Sal and Joey flooded her mind. She pushed those thoughts quickly aside. "Yeah, but not here. Can we go to your place?"

"We can go anywhere your little heart desires." Phil placed his arm around her waist. He guided her out of the park. She got into her car and followed him. *I can change my mind anytime.* Hunger grew inside of her. It was uncontrollable. All she wanted was a little break from this thing called life. What was the harm in that? *It doesn't make me a bad person.* Before she knew it, she had arrived at Phil's apartment.

"Come in... make yourself comfortable."

Vickie walked into the apartment. Her breathing labored, her step hesitant. She moved slowly toward the couch. Phil handed her a little plastic bag. She took out the powder and made lines on the coffee table. She took the rolled-up dollar bill from Phil. She snorted. Satisfaction followed.

"Hello... Yes it is... I don't understand... My wife never showed up?... Okay, I'll be right there." Sal looked at Margaret. "I gotta pick up Joey. Can you lock up everything? I won't be back."

"Sure... Sal... Is everything okay?" The anxiety in her voice was not lost on Sal.

"Yeah. Don't worry. I have to pick up Joey from school. Vickie didn't show up for some reason." He recognized the look on her face. "Just because she didn't pick him up doesn't mean she's back on drugs. She could be having one of her migraines. I'm sure she fell asleep and lost track of the time." Sal made an excuse.

"I've got things covered. See you tomorrow."

As Sal got into his car, he tried to call Vickie on her cell. He'd fed Margaret a tale that he didn't believe. "Vick. Where are you? You didn't pick Joey up from school. Are you okay? Call me!" He hung up the phone. Anger filled every part of his being. *She'd better have a great explanation as to why she forgot about our son.*

"How're you feeling baby?" Phil asked.

Vickie smiled with her eyes closed. "I feel great!... I haven't felt this great in a long time." Vickie could feel Phil's hand stroking her face. "Hmmm. I missed your touch."

"I miss yours too, baby." Phil bent forward. "Can I kiss you?"

Vickie opened her eyes. Phil looked at her with such care and tenderness. It moved her. "You can, but are you able?" She whispered. Phil leaned in close, kissed her tenderly at first then more aggressively. She responded passionately.

"Are you sure about this, baby?" He managed when he came up for air.

"I'm tired of being Mrs. Cleaver." She took off his shirt. She continued to kiss him like she was ravenous. "Take me to bed, Phil."

"Gladly." He picked her up in his arms and walked toward the bedroom.

"I'm glad you weren't scared, Buddy."

"I'm a big boy, Daddy."

"Yes, you are. Get your books out so I can help you with your homework."

"Okay, Daddy."

Where are you Vick? Oh God, please let her be all right. Why did he care? It was apparent she cared for no one but herself.

"I have to practice writing the letter N today. I can do it myself, Daddy."

"That's because you're a big boy, like you said. I'm going to be in here making dinner if you need my help."

Vickie sat up in bed. *Crap, look at the time.* She started putting on her clothes in a panic.

"Hey baby. Where's the fire? You don't have to leave you know."

"It's late. I forgot to pick up my son. He's probably home by now, and Sal will be furious. I've got to come up with a good story."

"Why not tell him the truth?"

She shook her head. "Don't be ridiculous. I can't do that."

"What about what happened between us?"

Vickie sighed. "Phil... that was *really* nice... but... it's not real. It was the drugs and nostalgia."

"Wow. I feel hurt... and used," he said as he covered himself with the sheets.

"Knock it off." She bent down and kissed him. "I didn't say I wouldn't come back." She smiled and left.

What in the hell are you going to say to Sal? She knew that whatever excuse she came up with had to be good, or else Sal would suspect she was lying.

"Good job, Buddy. You made perfect looking N's. Your teacher will love it."

"Thanks, Daddy." Sal heard the door. Vickie came into the kitchen. "Mommy's home!" Joey squealed.

"Hey, Baby. Mommy's sorry she didn't pick you up at school."

"It's okay. Daddy picked me up."

Sal noticed that her jeans were ripped and her clothes were dirty. "What happened to you Vick?"

"Joey, go inside. I want to talk to Daddy."

"Mommy you have a boo boo."

"Mommy's okay, Buddy. Go on and play." Joey skipped out of the kitchen toward his bedroom. "I'm so sorry, Sal. My cell phone died. I forgot to charge it before I left the house... Well anyway, I went for a walk in the park. I lost track of time and I noticed that it was getting late so I started to run towards the car. I fell down like an idiot. I hurt my knee and hit my head. I must of passed out or something..."

"Stop!" Sal said with his hand held up. He couldn't tolerate another word.

"Sal. You can't hold my getting hurt against me. After all, I went to the park in the first place to clear my head because you lied to me."

"You're being ridiculous."

"Where were *you* today?" she glared at him.

Sal swallowed hard. "I... I was at the store; then I went out for a cup of coffee. Wait a minute. This isn't about me. It's about you not showing up to pick up our son!"

"Right, coffee. Did you have coffee alone or did you have company?" She scowled.

He couldn't lie at this point. Not telling her was one thing but to straight out lie was something *she* did, not him. "I had coffee with Rose."

"So this morning when I asked you what you had planned for the day, you lied to me."

"I'm sorry. I shouldn't have lied." He walked over to her, placed his hands on her shoulders. There was an empty look in her eyes. It scared him. "Nothing is going on between us. We're just friends. As a matter of fact she's on a date tonight. She met someone and just wanted to talk about it."

"Then why lie?"

"I just didn't want to get into a fight this morning... but you're right. I won't withhold the truth from you again." He looked into her eyes. They were glassy. Was it because she had cried, or was high? "Did you really fall today?"

"Seriously. Look at me. Would I do this to myself?" A tear fell down her cheek.

Sal didn't know how to respond to her. Was her tear sincere or was she up to no good? "I guess not. Are you okay?"

"I am now. Eventually, someone walked by and helped me. I felt dizzy. As soon as I felt better, I drove home." She placed her arms around him and pulled him close. "I love you Sal; you know that, right?"

Sal wanted to believe her. When she kissed him, he felt it down to his toes. He loved her in spite of their troubles. When she kissed him like that nothing else mattered. He lost himself in her. "I love you too."

"Eww. Mommy and Daddy are kissing."

They both turned to see that Joey had entered the room. They chuckled. Sal scooped him up in his arms. "Eww, huh. Why don't we eat dinner?"

"Yeah! Dinner. No kissing."

Chapter 18

Rose sat opposite Jeremy at Bleu Nuit, a French restaurant located near Central Park. The intimate surroundings made her feel ill at ease. It had been a long time since Rose had been on a date. She kept her hands folded to stop them from shaking. If she were honest with herself, she had gone on this date to prove something to her family and to Sal. She had to prove she was ready to move on with someone. She felt the pressure to untangle how she felt about Sal. The small restaurant gave it a cozy feel. A dozen red roses adorned each of the ten tables. Crystal glasses, white china plates with small blue flowers, and blue linen tablecloth decorated each table. Bleu Nuit was well known for its French cuisine. The wait list was long, which made Rose wonder what type of connections Jeremy had to get a reservation on such short notice.

"Have you ever been here before, Rose?" he asked.

"No, I always wanted to, but reservations are hard to come by, and it's above my pay grade." Rose hoped that didn't sound obnoxious. She smiled at him.

"The hostess here is a childhood friend. We go way back. I called in a favor. I guess I wanted to impress you." Rose felt her cheek flush as if she was back in high school. "So did it work?" he asked.

"Yes, it did... so what do you recommend?" She wanted desperately to change the subject.

"They make excellent crepes here, both savory and sweet."

"I love crepes." As soon as the words came out of her mouth, Rose realized how high pitched her voice sounded. *Let's try some mature conversation.*

"Hey, it's okay. This is awkward for me too." They both chuckled. "The last time I went on a date was with my wife about a week before she died."

"Me too, I mean with Duane, my husband. It's much easier to

date someone you're already married to—no pressure." He shook his head in agreement. "Why don't we both give each other a break, and let's talk about them."

"You mean your husband and my wife."

"Yeah... That way we get it out of our system and maybe learn about each other in a more relaxed way."

"As friends first."

"Yes... so tell me about your wife?"...

By the time dinner was over Rose felt close to Jeremy. It was as if he could read her mind. She sipped her coffee and laughed. "I had the nicest time tonight," she said.

"Well the night is still young. I was thinking maybe we could go for a carriage ride around Central Park."

"I don't know." She wasn't sure why she was hesitant. She had had a good time so far.

"I promise no pressure, just a nice ride in the park."

"Okay. That sounds like fun."

"I'll pay on our way out." He rose and pulled out her chair.

"Thank you. I need some air, I'll meet you outside."

Rose stood in front of the restaurant and noticed a horse and carriage outside. *Did he plan this all along?* Jeremy came out of the restaurant and stood next to her.

"I was hoping you would want to go for a ride." He took her hand and led her to the carriage. She got in.

"It got chilly didn't it?"

"Here's a blanket... may I?" She nodded so he proceeded to pull the blanket over their legs. He moved in close to her. She felt her pulse race. He placed his arm around her shoulder. She wanted to run but talked herself out of it. She had to move on. Everyone told her she had to get on with life—her mom, her sister... Sal. Rose turned toward him. His eyes were warm and inviting. He leaned closer to her face and paused. "Rose, I want to kiss you so much right now... It's the first time since my wife died... I don't want to violate your boundaries." Her mind raced. *Why not?* She didn't say a word, but met his lips with hers. They kissed softly at first then with such eagerness it surprised her. He moved back slightly.

"Did I do something wrong?" she asked.

"You've done nothing wrong. I don't want to stop kissing you, Rose. I don't want to stop at... just kissing. It surprised me. I feel like I'm doing something wrong."

"I see."

"Maybe it would be best if I took you home now."

"Or maybe you can come up for a drink." He returned her smile and touched her cheek softly.

"You're a beautiful woman, Rose. From the first time I saw you... I was drawn to you. I wouldn't want to mess up whatever this is." He paused. "Are you sure about going to your apartment?"

"Let's discuss it over a drink."

"Sounds good to me."

Henry sat on his side of the bed. He tossed and turned for the better part of the night and finally gave up on his inability to sleep.

"Henry, are you all right?" Ida rolled over.

"Go back to sleep Ida. I'm fine."

"Henry James, you hush. I can tell you're not fine. Tell me why sleep escapes you."

"I couldn't sleep because it's about to come to a head. That young man is about to face a big challenge."

"Oh, Henry; that's awful. Anything I can do?"

"You can pray for him, Ida. Pray for me that I handle it the way the Lord would have me handle it."

"Henry, you always do the right thing. I'm surprised how you still doubt."

Henry faced Ida. Her eyes were so expressive. He had no doubt that she loved him. "Do you have any idea how much I love you?"

"Well, I'm pretty terrific." She smiled in that way that made his heart skip a beat.

"Yes you are, my dear, yes you are. I'll need to take a trip tomorrow, Ida."

"Will you be going far?"

"Just the hospital."

"Oh, Henry. Are you sick?"

"I'm just fine; it's just I need to visit someone there."

"Oh no… is that young man going to be hurt?"

"No Ida, it will be worse than that for him."

Chapter 19

Sal sat in his office as he stared at nothing in particular. When he had left this morning, Vickie seemed a bit too at ease. *What am I supposed to do? I love her even though she has put me through such heartache.* His thoughts then drifted to Rose. He had loved her once, but not in the way he came to love Vickie. In the beginning of his relationship with Vickie, he thought he had made a mistake. Now that Rose was back in his life, his feelings were conflicted. He wasn't sure whether it's real or just an escape from the hell he had to walk through these past few years. He's married—for better or worse, in sickness and in health... those words haunted him. He bit his nails until they bled. A nasty habit he had when he was nervous.

His cell phone vibrated. "Hello... Rose... how are you?" *Hmm. She sounded odd.* "So how did your big date go?... Oh... that's great... so glad you had a good time... I'd like to meet him sometime." He wasn't sure if he wanted to, but it seemed like the appropriate response. His phone buzzed again. He looked and it wasn't a number he recognized. "Rose, I got another call. I'll call you back." He hung up from Rose. "Sal Martinelli, can I help you?... Yes I'm his father... is something... what?... Where is he?... I'll be right there."

Rose skipped work the next morning. She didn't want to face herself, much less the people she worked with. Everyone would have asked her about her "big" date. *Why did I tell everyone about it?* She called Sal. *Why did I do that?* She knew the answer to her own question—she wanted to make him jealous. *What type of person pursues another woman's husband?* She knew her behavior was despicable. Last night proved it.

The doorbell rang. She sighed. It had to be either her mother or Candy. *Maybe I should have returned the plethora of calls they made.* If she had to choose, Candy would be better than her mom.

"I know you're home. Open up Rose," she heard her mother's voice through the door. She wasn't ready for this, but she had to face the music sooner or later.

"Coming." She opened the door. "Hello, *Mother.*" Lauren raised one eyebrow. "Sorry... come on in Mom."

"You don't look sick. I called you at work and they told me you called in sick. So what's up?" *I guess small talk is out of the question.*

What could she tell her? Sorry Mom, I had too much to drink, felt lonely, lusted after a married man, which led me to sleep with a man I barely knew. She hadn't slept with Duane before they were married or Sal when they were together in college. Maybe that's why she lost him back then. Her faith and values were important to her. *Where are those values now?* Just because his marriage was a mess didn't mean she could step in and take advantage. The guilt overwhelmed her.

Rose couldn't look her mom in the eyes. "Do you want some coffee? I just made some."

"Honey, I didn't come here for coffee. I can tell by the look on your face that something is wrong. Talk to me."

Rose grabbed her coffee cup and plopped down on the couch. Her mom followed and sat next to her. She gazed into her cup as if there would be magical words that would spring forth from the bottom. "Mom... I... I..." She couldn't say the words out loud. Rose couldn't bare her mother's disappointment. She imagined what she would say, *"Rose is that how your father and I raised you? I know you've been married and you're a grown woman, but it doesn't mean your values are gone with the wind. Just because times have changed doesn't mean you should."*

"Rose you're scaring me. What happened?"

"I... slept with him." Rose couldn't help but hide her face in her hands.

"Who did you sleep with?" Lauren asked.

Rose thought that was an odd question. "Jeremy after our date last night."

"Did he manipulate you in some way."

"No. Jeremy was kind and understanding... so polite. He never pushed. To the contrary, he asked me many times if I wanted him to leave or to stop, but to be honest I didn't. This morning in the light of day, I'm just ashamed."

"Rose, sometimes things happen, we make choices... mistakes... no one is perfect."

"I know Ma, but I feel like I'm such a loser."

"You're not a loser sweetheart. You made a mistake... Do you think this is too big for God to forgive? He loves you, baby. I hear that's His job to forgive people when they ask."

"It's just..."

"You knew it was wrong but did it anyway," she said without condemnation. She looked at her mom while her tears flowed freely. Lauren reached out to her. Rose placed her head on her shoulder. "I love you, Rose. Let me help you."

"Thanks for being here, Ma."

Sal was surprised he didn't get a speeding ticket on the way to the hospital. His mind raced as he ran inside. "I'm Sal Martinelli. I was told my son Joey was brought in. Where is he?"

"Let me look it up for you sir." It seemed as if she moved in slow motion. "Mr. Martinelli, he's in surgery right now."

"Surgery? What's going on? Is my wife here?"

"I'm not sure sir, but I'll take you to the waiting room, and I'll find someone who knows what's going on with your son."

She led him to a small room down the hall. Vickie was there. "Vickie." She looked at him with a tear-streaked face, "What happened?"

"It was such a nice day. I took him to the park... there was a car..."

"Vick! What happened to *my* son?" She was incoherent. "Are you high?"

"What?... No... " She slurred her words.

He grabbed her, shook her. "So help me Vickie if he doesn't... "

At this point a nurse came in, cleared her throat and stood until Sal turned around. He could just imagine what was on her mind when she walked into the room. "Sir, your son is still in surgery. He was struck by a hit and run driver. He lost quite a bit of blood."

"Does he need blood?"

"We're fine for now, but we are putting in a request for more. Your son has a very rare blood type AB-. Do you know what type you are?"

"Yeah, I'm O and his mother is AB." Sal didn't like the look on her face. "Is there something wrong? I would be happy to give blood."

"I... I don't think that will be necessary. As soon as the doctor is done, he'll come in and let you know how the surgery went. You can wait in here."

"Thank you." She looked at Vickie and then at Sal. When she turned to leave, Sal reached out and touched her on the arm. "Excuse me, nurse. Why did you give me that look?"

"I'm sorry sir. I didn't mean to give you a look."

"When I said I would give blood, you gave me a funny look when I told you our blood types." She wouldn't look at him.

"Sorry again. Just try to relax sir, I'll go see if there is another update."

Sal wasn't sure what the problem was, but he'd worry about that later. He wanted to strangle Vickie for not keeping a better eye on Joey. She's using again, and now his son is paying the price for his mercy towards her.

Nadine Zawacki

Chapter 20

As Sal paced back and forth in the small room, he shot looks of hatred towards Vickie. She wouldn't look at him. He could tell she started to come down from whatever high she was on. Sal hated himself for forgiving her again. He forgave plenty, but he drew the line when it came to Joey. Silence was better than the alternative thoughts going through his mind.

"Sal." He ignored her. "Sal, please look at me." He sighed, then turned around. "It wasn't my fault he got hit by a car."

"Really. Then whose fault would it be?"

"The hit and run driver," she stated plainly.

"I see. So what kind of car was it exactly that hit him?"

"I... didn't get a good look... it happened so fast... I was in shock."

"What color was the car?"

"I don't know! Stop bothering me with questions I don't know the answers to! What in the hell do you want from me?"
"Well for starters the truth. How could you let this happen to our son?"

"*Our* son?"

"Yeah, our son! What's wrong with you?"

"Nothing. I'm just tired."

"Well, you can answer my questions or the police's. The choice is yours."

"Police? You called the police?"

"No; they came by earlier, but you were out getting coffee. They said they would be back to ask you questions about what happened. My questions will seem like a spa day compared to the police. I'm not covering for you anymore."

Sal could see the panic set in, but he didn't care. All he cared about was Joey.

"Excuse me." Sal turned to find a doctor had entered the room. "Are you the Martinellis?"

"Yes," they said in unison.

"I'm Doctor Douglas. I just operated on your son. He's stable for now and you can see him as soon as they get him into a room. He's lost a lot of blood, and there were internal injuries. He ruptured his spleen, and I had to remove it."

"Is he going to be alright?" Sal asked dreading his response.

"The surgery went well. We just have to wait to see when he wakes up how he progresses."

Sal shook his hand. "Thank you, Doctor." Vickie rose and shook his hand. When the doctor left the room Sal followed behind him. "Excuse me, Doctor Douglas."

"Yes."

"May I ask you a quick question?"

"Certainly."

"If a child has AB-blood and his mother has AB blood and the father has O, is there a problem with that equation?"

"Well, a child with AB-blood would most likely have a parent with AB or A or B combination, but not O. That wouldn't add up."

"Thanks Doctor." Sal felt as if someone just plunged a knife in his heart and repeatedly turned it. Joey wasn't his son as he had been led to believe. Everything started to spin. His breathing was heavy. She had lied to him from day one. He went back into the waiting room. His mind was about to explode. He tried to remain calm, but a familiar voice bought him back to realty.

"Sal." He turned to find Mr. and Mrs. Delfeno. "We just heard on the news that there was an accident by the park close to the apartment. They didn't mention any names, but the way they described the child... we were afraid when we couldn't reach you that… Some of the tenants thought they saw Vickie at the scene. We came here to see for ourselves… Is he okay?" asked Mrs. Delfeno, who finally got to her point. She often rambled when she was upset.

This confrontation was something he didn't want to have in front of the Delfenos. "I think so. The Doctor said they had to remove his spleen, and he lost lots of blood. We haven't gotten a chance to see him yet."

"Is there anything we can do?" asked Mr. Delfeno.

"Not really, but thanks."

"How are you doing dear?" Mrs. Delfeno directed her question to Vickie.

"I'm fine. Excuse me. I need to go to the restroom."

As she passed by Sal, he reached out and held her arm. "Don't be long. We'll be able to see him soon."

Before she could leave the room a man stood at the entrance. He startled them. "Hello. My name is Detective Nelson. I'm here to investigate the hit and run on…" He checked his notepad. "Joey Martinelli. I understand his mother was with him."

Sal noticed the color drain from Vickie's face. He was determined to let her pay the piper. He still held her arm. He held on tightly so she couldn't escape. "This is Vickie, his mother. I'm Sal his… father."

"I'm sorry for what has happened to your son. I also have a son, and if this happened to him… anyway… Can you tell me what happened leading up to him getting hit by the car?"

Vickie looked at Sal. He just continued to hold on to her. "We were at the park. He was playing with his ball. He would throw it at me, and I would throw it back." She bit her lip. Sal wondered if this was true or did she make it up. "I guess I threw it and it rolled far… and then my phone rang… I… um… it happened so fast… he really knows better than to… but… I guess he ran after the ball into the street…"

"Take your time Mrs. Martinelli. I know how difficult this must be, but it's important that we act on it quickly before the driver's trail runs cold. Did you see what type of car it was? What color? License plate number... even a partial number... Anything that would help us to identify him or her?"

Sal enjoyed it a little too much as Vickie tried to squirm her way out of the detective's questions. "It happened so fast... I don't know anything about cars."

"Can you at least tell me the color or how big it was? Sometimes it helps when we ask around the scene of the accident if we have something to go by... no matter how small a detail."

"It was black and... a regular looking car... um... it wasn't big... just, um... regular size."

"Regular size... well then, here's my card in case you remember anything else that could help us." He handed Sal his card.

"Thank you... Excuse me, I was heading for the restroom." Sal let go of her arm. He had never seen her move so fast. He was about to follow her when the detective stopped him.

"Mr. Martinelli. Can I ask you a few questions?"

"I wasn't there. I was at work. I don't know what I could tell you."

"I just wanted to know if maybe your wife said anything to you that she may have forgotten? People get nervous when they talk to cops."

"No. She told you more than she told me." *Now's your opportunity Sal. All you have to do is tell this detective you thought Vickie was high at the time.*

"Okay then. Well, you have my number if you think of anything or you have any questions." He shook Sal's hand and gave him a caring look.

"Thank you, Detective."

Chapter 21

Mr. Delfeno entered the hospital room. Sal held Joey's hand as he sat next to his bed. "Excuse me, Sal." He looked up. "Marie and I looked everywhere, but couldn't find Vickie. She must have left the hospital."

"With all the problems Vickie and I have, the one thing I thought she cared about was Joey. What am I going to tell him when he asks for her?"

Before Mr. Delfeno could answer, Joey started to stir. "Mommy." He whispered quietly. Sal's heart quickly sank. He didn't want to disappoint his son.

"Hey, Buddy. I'm here... Daddy's here."

He blinked open his eyes. "It hurts, Daddy."

"Okay, Buddy. You relax, and I'll get a doctor or nurse to help you."

"Don't leave me, Daddy." His eyes were dejected, filled with fear.

"It's okay. I'm going to press this button, and the nurse will come. I'm not going anywhere."

The nurse responded shortly. She was a young woman with bright red hair and freckles. She smiled as she asked, "How are you doing?"

"He said it hurts," Sal replied for him.

"He's due for some medication." She checked his vital signs. Sal watched as she probed and prodded. "Everything looks good. I'll be right back with medication and let the doctor know he's awake."

"Thanks. See, Buddy, it's going to be okay."

"Can I get you anything, Sal?"

"No thank you, Mr. Delfeno. I've got what I need right here."

Vickie could take care of herself. He had to concentrate on Joey. How much was he required to forgive?

Vickie was sweating and her breathing arduous. She banged on Phil's door, but he didn't answer. "Where in the hell are you?" *Doesn't he know she needs him... she needs something right now.* She sat down on the floor by the door with her knees bent. With her elbows on her knees she placed her face in her hands. Vickie sat in that position for what felt like an eternity.

"Hey, you okay?"

She was startled by the unfamiliar voice. When she looked up she saw a sketchy looking young man with a blue Mohawk. He was wearing torn jeans, a skull and cross bones T-shirt, and dark glasses. "I'm waiting for my friend," Vicki answered.

"You mean Phil?"

"You know him?" Vickie asked astonished. It's New York. Most people don't know their neighbors, much less by name.

"Well yeah, he's an *associate* of mine," he answered as he licked his lips just like Phil. "Are you a customer of his private business dealings?"

Vickie wasn't sure what she should do. She wasn't sure where Phil could be and how long it would take him to get home. "I can wait for Phil."

He bent down close her face. She scooted back against the door.

"Are you sure? If you're a friend of Phil's then you're a friend of mine."

"I don't have any money on me." She volunteered.

"I'm sure we can work *something* out," he said with an evil smirk on his face. "Come on. I have what you need at my place. It's just down the hall."

He extended his hand to her as he stood up. Vickie took his

hand and got up from the floor. She's done worse for a hit. This guy was at least good looking in his own way. She thought his colored Mohawk suited him. "Hey, Vickie, where are you going?" She turned around. It was Phil.

"I... I was waiting for you."

Phil looked the young man over. "What do you think you're doing, Porter?"

"Hey man, I was just trying to help a lady out."

"Get lost. This one is *mine*. Nobody touches her. Are we clear?"

"Yeah, man." Vickie's hand was still in his so he kissed it. "Sorry baby, but the King has spoken. I'll catch you next time, my lady." Porter raised his hands in surrender. He continued down the hall.

"Don't make me hurt you, Porter," Phil snapped.

"Enough said, man," Porter replied.

"Vickie what's wrong with you. You know better than that. Why didn't you just call me, baby?"

"Oh Phil," was all Vickie managed to say before she grabbed him and started to cry.

"Now, now... don't get upset. Phil's got something to make you feel better. Let's go inside."

Sal sat on a pew in the hospital chapel. Mrs. Delfeno was with Joey while he slept. He needed some guidance... some direction. It was peaceful in the chapel. It wasn't very large. There were only five rows of pews, a wooden cross at the front of the room and three candles of varying heights resting on two small tables on either side. His whole world was coming apart at the seams. He had no idea where Vickie was, and, to be honest, he didn't care. The son he loved more than life itself was not his biological son. He had never felt so alone. All the times that Vickie left and went back to Phil, at least he had Joey. It didn't change his heart towards his son, but did it mean she could take him away? *Over his dead body!* He heard the door open behind him. The old man who entered sat down next to him. He thought that was awkward since the rest of the chapel was empty.

"Hello," said the old man.

"Hello," Sal responded back. "I hate to be rude, but I would rather be alone."

"I know, but I was sent here to see you."

Great! The last thing he needed was to be seated next to a crazy old man who escaped from the psych ward. "Do I know you?" *Don't humor him.*

"No, but I know of you," he smiled. "Let me explain. I'm on a mission from God." *Yep, the psych ward had an escapee.* "My name is Henry James. God speaks to me sometimes and told me about you, your wife, and your little son. He got hurt badly today. Your wife is lost, and now you're questioning your faith." *Who is this guy?*

"What? Who's been talking to you? How do you... how do you know these things?"

"I told you, God speaks to me. I have a message for you, if you want it."

Sal didn't know what to make of this whole situation. If his day wasn't bizarre enough, he now faced a man who thinks God spoke to him. "My wife is a drug-addicted whore. It's her fault my son got hit by a car, and to make matters worse, she ran off *again*. What type of message can help me with that?"

Henry looked him in the eyes. Compassion stared back at him. "I know I may sound like a crazy old man, but it doesn't change the fact that I hear from God. You just found out today that your son is not your blood. He's another man's child. You know whose child he is, don't you?"

What this man spoke to him was truth that he hadn't uttered to anyone else. Tears filled his eyes and trickled down his cheeks. He didn't know what to say or how to respond.

"God loves you," Henry said softly.

"I don't feel loved."

"I'm here to tell you that He does love you. He also loves your wife. She's just lost her way. She's felt alone and unwanted all her life. She's made wrong choices just to mask her pain. I'm not making excuses for her, mind you, just stating the facts as I'm aware of them. Do you think it was a mistake you found her on that bench?"

"What... wait... how did..."

"I only know what God wants me to know. Where do you think your love for her comes from? She needs you. Your son needs you. He has been and always will be your son. You may not have had a hand in his creation, but you have a hand in the man he will be one day. With you as his father he will grow up to be a good man. He will never feel alone or abandoned."

"She doesn't love me. I've tried, but she doesn't love me back." Sal couldn't hold back any longer. He wept. There was something about this man that felt safe. Henry put his arm around him. He felt peace flow from his embrace. Sal didn't understand what was going on, but a calm came over him as his tears subsided.

"She loves you; she doesn't know it yet. You need the strength to fight for her and your family. It's going to get a little worse before it gets better. Keep in mind that few things can dull the senses and distort perception as thoroughly as an offense. Don't give up... May I pray for you?"

Sal shook his head. Words escaped him. Henry started to pray. His words were simple but powerful. Sal wasn't sure what had just happened, but he was grateful. For the first time he felt God cared. He cared enough to send someone to help. He wasn't sure he was worthy, but he was grateful.

Nadine Zawacki

Chapter 22

Rose was done beating herself up about her night with Jeremy. She stood at the foot of Joey's bed as he slept. Sal sat next to his bed with Joey's hand in his. The pain in Sal's eyes was sobering. Her problems seemed minute in comparison. "Sal... Sal." He didn't turn to look at her. She walked over to him and placed a hand on his shoulder. It startled him.

"Rose, I'm sorry. I forgot you were here."

"Don't worry yourself about me; I'm fine. Can I get you anything?"

"No thanks..."

"When was the last time you ate something?"

"I'm not hungry."

"Well, I understand that, but I'm going to get you something anyway. You won't do Joey any good if you're too weak to take care of him."

"Maybe later."

"I hate to bring up a sore subject but..."

"You mean Vickie." He said her name void of emotion. "I have no idea... no, that's not true. If I know her, she's probably with that drug dealer. She usually runs to him... for comfort."

"I'm sorry Sal. If there is anything I can do for you... or Joey?" Rose's cell phone rang. "I'm sorry, I forgot to turn it off." Rose noticed that Jeremy called. She sent him a quick text to let him know she will call later.

"You can go if you need to. I'll be all right."

"I'm going to get you something to eat. No arguments."

Sal smiled. "Thanks, Rose. You're a good friend."

Rose walked out of the room. Jeremy had responded to her text. It made her blush slightly. *How are you going to explain to him about the other night being a one-time deal?* She had learned something from this whole experience. She was lonely. She didn't handle it well. It was loneliness that awoke old feelings for Sal. It was loneliness that led her to have sex with Jeremy. *I'm sorry, Lord, for filling my loneliness with everything else but You. Show me how to make this right.*

Vickie lay on Phil's bed covered in nothing but a thin sheet. The euphoric feeling she had had fleeted quicker than she wanted. Reality crept in like a slap on the face. Sal would never forgive her for Joey being hurt. Being high made it all go away... at least temporarily. She wished she could stay that way all the time. The numbness made life bearable. Phil walked in with a tray in his hands.

"Hey Baby, I heated up some food for you. I had some left over pasta from dinner last night."

"I'm not hungry. I really should go."

"You don't have to go anywhere, baby. You're welcome to stay here." He placed the tray down on a table. He sat down on the bed next to her and placed his hand on her leg. She felt dirty. "What's wrong?" Phil asked.

"I want to see my kid."

"Hey, you're free to do whatever you want. I don't own you."

Vickie chuckled. "Of course you do. You've always owned me. That's why I keep coming back."

Phil's cell phone rang. He looked at it and then excused himself. Vickie wondered what that was about. He had an evil look on his face when he looked at his phone. *What are you up to now Phil?* She located her clothes and got dressed.

"Going somewhere?"

"I'm going to the hospital."

"You're sure that's a good idea?" Phil asked.

"I don't know, but I have to see him."

"*Him?*... Do you mean Sal or Joey?"

"It doesn't matter."

"Do you want me to come with you?"

Vickie shook her head. "Don't be stupid. Sal would take your head off."

"Really, now." Phil laughed. "That weak husband of yours hasn't had the guts to touch me yet. You think he would lay a hand on me? That's rich, baby."

"He's not weak!" she protested. Suddenly she felt protective—a reaction that surprised her.

"Those are your words, baby, not mine. You've said 'em hundreds of times and worse in the past."

"You can be really cruel at times." Phil came over to her and took hold of her arm. He squeezed it tightly. "Let go of me!"

"How much longer do you think I'm going to let you do this to me?"

"Do what?" she shot back repulsed.

"Use me!... for drugs?... for sex? Whenever you get bored with being a wife and mother, you come crawling back to me."

She slapped him with her free hand. He hadn't expected her to do that. He let her go. "I'm sick. There's no other explanation."

"No... I'm the one who's sick. The things I do for you, you don't even know."

"What things?

"Never mind. You just remember one thing, baby; I'm the only one who has what you need. I'm the only one who understands you. That husband of yours wants to fill your life with the ordinary... the mundane. I want to give you excitement. If you leave him, I would show you the world."

"What about Joey?"

"Hey, baby, I know he's mine. We could bring him with us if you want. Maybe it's time he learns who his *real* father is. I've saved up a nice little sum of money. We could go anywhere you want—a fresh start. Doesn't that sound nice, baby?"

"I won't do that to Joey! Sal's the only father he's ever known."

"Then leave him with Sal. We could start a new family."

"Really?"

"Anything for you, baby."

"You don't care about anyone but yourself, Phil. Let's be real... you're dangerous. That might be okay for me, but not for a kid. I need a fresh start all right, but not with you." Phil looked into her eyes. She felt chills go throughout her body. "I gotta go, Phil."

"You tell yourself what you need in order to sleep at night, but I know the truth."

Vickie turned around. "Your truth... please."

"No baby... *the* truth. The truth is I'm the only man who ever really loved you. I know what you need, what you like... I've taken care of you, and I'm the one who you keep coming back to. Deep down you love me and only me. Sal is safe, and let's face it—you're not attracted to that no matter how much you have tried to convince yourself."

Vickie couldn't take it anymore. She couldn't breathe. She had to leave. She had to go and see her family. She had to get away from Phil.

Chapter 23

"Daddy..."

"What is it, Buddy?"

"Where's Mommy?" Joey asked. Sal looked upon him with sadness. What was he to tell his son? What excuse can he come up with that he hasn't used before? *Sorry, son, your Mom's probably high and in another man's bed.* Before he could say a word, he heard her voice.

"Mommy's here, little man." Vickie appeared in the doorway. He couldn't believe her audacity to show up like she had just stepped out to get some fresh air.

"Mommy! I hurt." Sal was amazed by Joey's ability to share both elation and pain within seconds of each other.

"My poor baby. Mommy's sorry she wasn't here when you woke up."

"I missed you."

"Vickie. May I have a word?" Sal said with more disdain than he intended.

"I don't want to leave Joey."

"That's rich." Vickie glared at him, but he was undeterred. "Hey, Buddy, we'll be right back."

"Okay, Daddy."

Vickie kissed Joey on the head. "We're just going to be right outside, okay? So if you need us, we'll be able to hear you."

They stepped outside the room and Sal spoke very softly. "You have something to tell me?"

"I'm really sorry Sal," she said. Sal thought she almost sounded sincere.

"You're *really* sorry. Well then all's forgiven and everything is fine."

"I wish it was. I know I messed up... badly this time." Sal saw a tear run down her cheek. In all the time that he knew her, he never saw her cry. The words of the old man he met came back to him. *You need strength to fight for her and to fight for your family.* Sal wasn't sure if he had any fight left in him.

"Seriously? You're unbelievable. Where were you?" Sal asked, but was afraid of the answer.

Vickie looked around not wanting to look at Sal directly. "Sal... I'm sorry."

"Never mind!" Sal walked back into the room. He was too upset to deal with her right now. He unfortunately recognized that glassy look in her eyes. All that changed when he looked at Joey. His heart melted. Vickie followed close behind and sat next to Joey's bed. Sal resented how she waltzed back into the room like everything was normal. He knew where she'd been and whom she was with even if she didn't say it out loud. *How could he fight for her when she pushed him away?*

"If you want to take a break Sal, I'll stay here with Joey."

"I'm not going anywhere," he snapped.

"If I remember correctly, you love pastrami..." Rose walked into the room and stopped short when she saw Vickie.

Vickie glared at her. "Rose, right? We kinda met a long time ago. I'm Vickie... *Sal's wife.*"

"When it's convenient." Sal mumbled under his breath. He felt ill at ease with both Rose and Vickie in the same room. "Thanks for stopping by, Rose. I appreciate the sandwich." Rose handed Sal a paper bag.

"No problem... If I had known you were here, Vickie, I would've gotten you something as well... well... anyway... um... I gotta go..."

"A hot date?" Vickie asked sarcastically.

Rose blushed, but didn't address her comment. "Feel better,

Joey. I'm praying for you."

"Thank you." Joey smiled.

"I'll walk you out, Rose." Sal saw the disapproval on Vickie's face. He didn't care if she was mad. "I'll be right back, Bud." He followed Rose out of the room. They walked silently until they reached the elevator. As they waited, Sal broke the silence first. "Thanks for the pastrami. You're a good friend, Rose."

"You're welcome. I was hoping you still loved pastrami on rye. There's also a dill pickle and a coke." She smiled.

"What can I say? I'm a creature of habit." He smiled. "So... do you have a hot date tonight?"

"I'm meeting Jeremy downstairs. Do you want to meet him?"

Sal thought about it for a moment when the elevator opened up. "I should get back to Joey. Maybe some other time."

Rose stepped into the elevator. "I hope that Joey gets to go home soon."

"Me, too," Sal said pensively.

"Maybe we could have coffee sometime."

"Of course. I'll call you when things settle down with Joey." Sal turned around to walk away.

Rose held the door to the elevator open. "Sal... I want to tell you that I'm not confused anymore."

"Confused?"

"About us. Friendship is our bond... nothing more. I appreciate that friendship."

"So do I, Rose... I'll see you soon." He had come to the same conclusion about their relationship. His trouble with Vickie sidetracked him a bit. Maybe with the confused feelings out of the way, true friendship could be established.

"See ya." Rose smiled and waved her hand.

Sal stood there for a moment. He wasn't sure how to repair his family. *Well you're not going to fix anything just standing here.*

He headed back to the room. He could hear Vickie's voice as he approached.

"So the pirate landed on the shores of Quincy, a far-away land. The pirate was looking for buried treasure. He had a map and couldn't wait to see if treasure would be his reward."

"What kind of treasure Mommy?"

"Gold coins, diamonds, rubies and pearls. The pirate took out his map to see where "X" marked the spot. His men with shovels in their hands followed close by as he searched for the big weeping willow tree... "

As Vickie continued her story, Sal remembered one of the reasons why he loved her. *With all her faults, Vickie loved Joey.*

Chapter 24

It had been about a month since Rose had heard from Sal. She was busy with her new relationship with Jeremy, and Sal was busy with his family. She missed his friendship. She wasn't sure what was wrong with her today, but her stomach felt queasy. *Oh no!* Rose rushed to the bathroom and just made it. She felt slightly better after she threw up. Maybe it was something she had eaten. She heard the doorbell. "Coming!" she shouted.

She staggered toward the door. She opened it up to find Candy. "Hey, Sis, you look like crap," she said as took off her shades.

"Love you too." Candy walked in. "Come in," Rose uttered after the fact.

"What gives, Rosie? You look all pale and stuff. Are you feeling okay?"

"I just threw up."

"Hmm. Bad shrimp?"

"No... Maybe... I think I'm coming down with something."

Candy chuckled. "If you were anyone else, I would have asked if you were pregnant." Rose lost more color in her face, if that were possible. She stared into space and sat down right where she stood. "Rosie... what's wrong?" Candy knelt beside her.

"Oh my God, Candy. I think I'm in trouble."

"Trouble? What are you talking about? What kind of trouble?"

"I..." she got up quickly and rushed back to the bathroom where she threw up again. Candy came in and bent down. Rose, overcome with fear, started to cry. "I think I could be pregnant." Candy roared. "I'm not joking." Rose added.

Candy's face changed. "You mean you and..."

"Jeremy."

"Whoa... oh. I didn't know you'd changed that much, Sis."

Rose got up from the floor. "Well, that's a response I would expect from Mom."

"Sorry... I didn't mean to be such a witch."

"Hey, that's the least of my problems... Look... I was lonely and it happened... once." Rose tried to justify her actions to her sister.

"Does Mom know?"

"Yes... not about possibly being pregnant, but about sleeping with Jeremy."

"Wow. She never told me anything. So how pregnant are you?"

"I'm not sure if I am. I haven't taken any tests. I just never thought about it until..."

"Until I opened up my big mouth."

Rose took Candy's hand. "No. That's not what I was going to say." She smiled at her sister. "Don't say anything to Mom until I know for sure."

"I promise... Hey, I'll go to the pharmacy and get you a test. There's no time like the present... I'm really sorry about my crack before. It was mean and hurtful."

"Thanks, Candy. I really need you. You're a good sister."

"Good... please, I'm the best sister you have."

"You're my only sister." Rose laughed.

"That's just a technicality. If we had more sisters, I still would be the best." Candy retorted.

Sal walked into the apartment at lunchtime. He wasn't sure if Vickie would be there, but he was tired of walking on eggshells since Joey's accident. "Vickie! Are you home?" She came out of the kitchen.

"Hey... What are you doing home?" she asked as she entered the room.

"We need to talk."

"About what?"

"Don't play dumb... About us."

"Oh," she said, as she looked downward.

"I love you Vickie." She didn't respond. "Can you say the same about me?"

"I don't... know what to say really."

"A good place to start would be that you love me too... Do you even want to be married?"

"Sal... it's just so hard. You won't let me be me."

"What? Are you kidding me? Let you be you. What does that even mean? If that means I won't let you be a drug-addicted whore, then no, you're right." As soon as the words came out of his mouth Sal regretted it. He had gotten used to calling her that for so long, it just slipped out. How he managed to say the wrong thing astonished him. Her words wounded him and in turn he wounded her. It wasn't a proud moment. His intentions didn't seem to matter at the time. *Why can't you just show her more love than hate?*

"I guess I deserve that. What about you, Sal?"

"What about me?" Sal shook his head.

"Have you slept with Rose?"

"I've never slept with her, not even in college! I haven't even seen or talked to her since she stopped by the hospital. Can you say the same about Phil?"

Vickie looked at Sal void of any emotion. He wondered if she had taken something. "Do you really want to know the answer to that?" Sal felt the chill of her words.

"What can I do Vickie? I have no pride left. I've tried to make you happy, but if you want to go to Phil and get high... then there's nothing I can do about it, but that's no life for a child. My son will stay with me."

An evil grin came over Vickie's face. "*Your* son. I know you know better than that Sal. I overheard you ask the doctor about blood types. Let's not pretend anymore shall we?" She walked over to him and leaned very close to him. She looked up at his face. "Who's the daddy?... Not you."

Sal wanted to kill her. He took a deep breath. "I'm the one listed on the birth certificate and the only one he knows. He will always be *my* son!"

"You're such a Boy Scout, aren't, you Sal? I knew that day when you found me on the park bench that I'd hit pay dirt."

"You knew you were pregnant that day?"

"Yep. I hadn't told the *real* father, but after minutes of meeting you, I knew you would step up to the plate."

"Shut up!" he yelled. "I can't believe you hate me this much."

Vickie sighed. For a slight moment he thought he saw her waiver in her resolve. "I don't hate you Sal. I... I pity you."

"Fine! Then leave... just without Joey."

"He's mine."

"No! He's mine. No judge on earth would give custody to a drug-addicted mother. So I suggest you pack your things and go back to the man who you think can give you what you need." Sal was furious. He was beyond hurt. How many times had he given her an ultimatum? How many times did he have to be belittled by her?

"Really, now."

"Don't mistake my mercy towards you as weakness. I tried to make this marriage work, but you don't seem interested. So you can leave. Having you here is not good for Joey. It's not good for... anybody. I know deep down you know this."

Vickie walked away and went into the bedroom. She came back out immediately with a bag in her hand. I was just waiting for you to come to the same conclusion I did. Goodbye, Sally." She slammed the front door on her way out.

Sal stood there in the empty apartment. *How long had she planned this? Joey. I've got to get to the school before she does.*

Nadine Zawacki

Chapter 25

Sal reached Joey's school just as it was letting out. His heart raced. He wasn't sure if Joey would be there, or if he was too late. He wouldn't put it past her to be vindictive even though Joey would cramp her style. Sal couldn't breathe. The lump in his throat expanded, as time seemed suspended. Sal anxiously searched the sea of children. When he spotted Joey, he was beyond relieved. Time resumed once again. Sal ran to him and picked him up in his arms.

"Daddy!"

"Hey, Buddy. How was school today?"

"Great! My teacher let me take a long nap. I was tired." Joey responded as he hugged Sal. "Where's Mommy?"

"She went on a trip. It's just going to be you and me for a while."

Without missing a beat Joey said, "Can we have pizza for dinner?" What a shame his mother's absence from his life was so normal that he didn't give it a second thought. The explanation he gave Joey was sufficient. He used it many times before. Vickie just left and he had no idea for how long or if he would take her back if she did. *Who are you kidding Sal, you would take her back in an instant.* Deep down Sal loved Vickie even after she had lied to him about Joey's paternity. Phil was Joey's biological father, a fact that killed him more than anything. There were days he could just scream. There was a war going on in his heart, mind and soul. Which part would win, he wasn't sure? He was determined no matter what that Joey wasn't going to be on the losing side.

"We can have pizza for dinner, but after you do your homework. How about we stop by the coffee shop so Daddy can get a coffee and I'll get you a fruit smoothie."

"Yeah! Any flavor I want?"

"Of course. Whatever you want."

Rose sat across Jeremy in the coffee shop. They must have sat there for several minutes without speaking.

"Are you nervous about something Rose?" he asked as he reached over and placed his hand gently on hers.

Rose hadn't realized she was tapping her nails on the table until Jeremy's hand touched hers. She giggled nervously. "Yeah... I'm not sure how to say this."

"Are you breaking up with me?" A look of panic crossed his face.

"No... no... you see..."

"Look Rose, I don't want to make you feel uncomfortable. We could just enjoy our coffee... well, in your case tea..." He smiled.

Rose realized what a sweet, kind and patient man he had turned out to be. Since their discussion about taking things slower, he had understood more than she had expected. Most men might have thought she was fickle and leave. Now she had to tell him he was about to be a father. "You're a nice guy..." She was about to just spill it when she spotted Sal enter with his son. She waved to him, but when he turned to look at her, his face turned white. She was confused when he stormed over to them. She had never seen rage before in his eyes, and it gave new meaning to the phrase, *if looks could kill.* Before she could say anything, Sal shouted at Jeremy.

"What in the hell are you doing here?" Sal spoke directly to Jeremy.

Confused, Rose asked, "You know Jeremy?"

Sal's head spun quickly in her direction. "What?"

"This is Jeremy. Sal, why are you so angry? Why are you yelling at him?"

"Hello," Joey said to Jeremy.

Sal looked down at his son. "Joey, you know this man?"

"Yes Daddy, this is Mommy's friend who bought me ice cream at the zoo... oops... that's a secret."

"Could someone please tell me what's going on here?" Rose asked. She felt self-conscious because people started to stare.

"That is not Jeremy! His name is Phil, as in the Slime-Ball-Drug-Pusher that my wife can't seem to stay away from!"

"Daddy... Daddy why are you yelling at Mommy's friend?" asked Joey.

"I'm sorry, Buddy. This is a bad man. He is nobody's friend. You should never go anywhere with him. Do you understand?"

"Yes, Daddy."

Rose suddenly felt like the ground opened up and swallowed her whole. She thought she would throw up right there. She looked at Jeremy whose whole complexion changed. If evil had a face she had just looked into its eyes. Before she asked, she knew the answer. "Is this true?"

"I'm afraid so, Sweetie."

"Get out of here!" Sal yelled.

"Daddy... Daddy." Joey cried as he tugged on Sal's pants. Sal picked up his son and held him in his arms. "I'm sorry for yelling, son. Daddy's sorry. It's going to be okay."

"Hey, man, don't get the kid so upset with your hostility... I guess the jig is up. Got to go anyway. I have company staying at my place." He winked at Sal. "Rose, my dear, it's been real. Thanks for the laughs. You rocked my world that night. I'll never forget you."

Phil stood up, saluted them, and then he left. Rose sat numb. She looked up at Sal—lost and confused at what just happened. Tears welled up in her eyes.

"Let's get out of here Rose." She couldn't move. "Rose, please come with me. We'll go back to my place where we can talk privately."

"Why? Why would he do that?"

"He's a sick man. Who knows why he does anything? I'm sorry, Rose, you got dragged into my mess."

Rose stood up but felt queasy. "Excuse me," she managed to utter before she headed to the bathroom. She made it just in time. When she was finished, she washed her face off with some cool water. She wished that there was such a thing as a transporter and all she had to do was ask Scotty to beam her up. "Pull yourself together, Rose. You have to go out there and face Sal." When she opened the door, Sal's look of anger was replaced by concern.

"Are you okay?"

"Yeah. I'm going home. I need to be alone."

"Oh... I understand. When you're up to it, we need... or if you want to talk about it... whatever you want."

On his drive home, Phil was quite content with himself. He had pulled it off. He had managed to derail Sal once again. He wondered what Rose wanted to tell him before they were interrupted? Maybe she was about to declare her love for him? *Ha! It doesn't matter now.* He couldn't wait to get back to Vickie so he could tell her what he had done for her. He made her care for him and kept her away from Sal at the same time. The important part was he was able to take her rival down a peg or two.

Chapter 26

Rose drove around town not knowing where to go or what to do next. She found herself in front of her mother's house. She sat in her car and wept. She wasn't sure how long she sat there, when she heard a light tap on the window. Lauren stood there with tears in her eyes and tissues in her hand. Rose stepped out of the car. Lauren extended her arms while Rose took a tissue.

"Oh, Ma, I've screwed up this time something fierce."

Lauren held her tightly. "My precious girl. Come inside, and we're talk about it if you want."

"Thanks." As they walked into the house Rose composed herself in order to speak. "Ma, Jeremy is not who he said he is."

"He's not?"

"I..."

"Sit. I'll make some tea."

Rose sat at the kitchen table while Lauren put water on for tea. Her mother always made mint tea during a crisis. She thought mint tea healed everything—a cold, a stomachache or a broken heart. As she prepared the tea, Rose had the time she needed to formulate her thoughts. Lauren placed two teacups down with a plate of cookies in the middle. Rose appreciated how astute her mother was. She knew when to speak and when to listen. "I love you, Rose, more than words can express. Nothing you could tell me would change that."

"Jeremy lied. He set me... no, I need to take responsibility for my own actions."

"First tell me what Jeremy did? How did he lie to you?"

Rose told her mother who Jeremy was and his history with Sal. At times she stopped to cry, but her mother encouraged her to continue. She finished up the story with what happened at the coffee shop. "I've made things worse for Sal." Rose stated matter-of-factly. She felt numb from rehashing everything.

"Rose you can't worry about Sal right now. You need to concern yourself with your unborn child."

"Duane wanted children so much and now I'm pregnant with a monster's baby. I'm so glad I didn't get a chance to tell Phil about it."

"Rose, it's not this child's fault who his/her father is. What matters now is that you protect your baby, my grandchild, from the evils of this world."

"How can I face people?" Rose asked.

"Really, Rose, that's the least of your concern. It doesn't matter what people think. If anyone gives you a hard time, just let me know. I'll set them straight. Besides, it only matters what God thinks."

Rose couldn't look her mother in the eyes when she spoke, "Yeah, I'm sure He's thrilled with me too."

Lauren shook her head. "Rose I don't want to sound like I'm just making light of your situation, but God loves you more than I do. He forgives you. What matters now is that you have this child inside of you. This child is not a mistake." Lauren placed her hand on Rose's. "You'll love this baby no matter who the father might be. You won't be alone. We'll help you every step of the way. I'm already madly in love with the little peanut."

She wasn't sure if she believed what her mother said about God. She didn't feel worthy. Her heart needed to believe that God forgave, even if her head wondered how He could. "How did I get so blessed to have a mom like you?"

"I am pretty terrific, but that's not the point. The point is that you're an amazing woman, and you'll be a great mom."

Sal waited outside Rose's apartment door. She didn't answer the door when he knocked. He wasn't sure if she was home so he sat down outside the door to wait for her. Joey was with the Delfenos. He knew Joey would be safe with them. He instructed Mr. Delfeno not to open the door to Vickie or let Joey leave with her. Mrs. Delfeno promised to call if Vickie showed up. He needed to see if Rose was okay. Phil sought Rose out, pretended to be someone else just to inflict pain and suffering—how despicable. He hadn't realized how much he had become dependent on her friendship. He sat there outside her door when he heard, "Sal, what are you doing here?"

Sal looked up. Rose stood above him. She looked disheveled. He stood up. "I know you said you wanted to be alone, but I was worried about you," he said as he stood up.

She didn't look at him as she placed the key in the door. "Sal... I don't know what to say." He saw tears well up in her eyes.

"I don't want to upset you. I just want to say how sorry I am for what has happened. It's all my fault."

"No it's not," she retorted.

"If it wasn't for me, he wouldn't have targeted you."

"How's Joey?" she asked to change the subject he thought.

"He's okay... he's safe. Thanks for asking."

Rose broke down. "Come in." Sal walked in and was heartbroken that the pain she felt was because of him. He waited until Rose continued. "I want to tell you something, but it's so hard... I'm... I'm going..."

"Rose, you don't have to tell me anything. You're a good woman that dated the wrong guy. I don't know..."

Rose blurted, "I'm pregnant." Sal wasn't sure he heard her correctly, but then she repeated it slower, "I'm pregnant."

Sal sat down at this point for the first time since he had walked into her apartment. He couldn't believe Phil had fathered yet another child. Tears trickled down her cheeks. "Does he know?"

"No. You came in when I was about to tell Jer... I mean Phil, that I was going to have a baby. It only happened once during a point when I felt lonely and sad... oh, Sal, that's just an excuse. It's my fault, but I can't tell that man... after what you've told me..."

"I know. I'm sorry." Sal felt a tear run down his cheek. "What are you going to do?"

"I'm going to have the baby, of course, but other than that I'm not sure. I don't want him to have anything to do with this baby. He's just a horrible, evil man."

"Makes you wonder why Vickie keeps going back to him."

"I don't understand that when she has someone like you." She smiled.

"I love her. I believe she loves Joey, but she loves Phil and drugs more."

Rose shook her head. "She doesn't love Phil. He's just a means to her real love—drugs. She's dependent on him, but not in love."

"It doesn't seem that way."

"Then why does she keep coming back to you? If she loved him, she would stay with him. He can give her what she wants most—escape. But what he can't give her is a family."

Sal had never thought of it that way. What if what Rose had said was right? He had to fight for her. He couldn't give up on her. Not now, not ever. "Rose you amaze me. This child is so lucky to have you as his mother."

"I only wish he had a different father."

"I get it, but you don't have to ever tell him. Trust me he's not interested in being a father."

"How do I get around my baby's curiosity when he starts school and people ask him about his father. My dad is a drug-dealing double-crossing son of a bitch who lied to my mother and pretended he was someone else and she was stupid enough to fall for it, slept with him; then, voila, I came to be."

They chuckled. It relieved the tension.

"I'm sorry. I know it's not funny, but I'm sure you'll come up with something."

"You're right. Now I just have to worry about keeping him safe."

"You're not alone. If there is anything I could do..."

"Thanks, you're a good friend... now go... get your wife away from that wicked man. Don't let her be lost to that world. She needs you, Sal."

"But she doesn't want me, Rose."

"Drugs do terrible things to people. She doesn't know what she wants. You just need to help her see that she loves you, too." She made sense in a strange way. All these years he'd tried over and over to make her see how much he loved her, but had never tried to show her that she loved him, too.

Nadine Zawacki

Chapter 27

Sal arrived at Phil's without a plan. *What if she didn't want to come home with him?* The thought dawned on him as he banged on the door. It didn't matter, because he was determined to get Vickie away from him.

"Open this door now! I know she's in there. I'm not leaving until I talk to my wife."

The door swung open quickly, which startled Sal. He hadn't faced Phil since he had confronted him at the coffee house. Phil had a smug look on his face, which Sal wanted to wipe from his face. "You're too late. She's not here."

Sal pushed his way into the apartment. "Mind if I don't take *your* word for it?" He looked around. The place was a mess. He saw Vickie's bag and picked it up. "So she's not here. Right, that's why her stuff is here."

Phil shrugged his shoulders and plopped on the couch amidst Vickie's things. "She left in a hurry. I'm not sure if she's coming back."

Sal grabbed Phil by his shirt with both hands and pulled him to his feet. "Listen to me you-drug-pushing-piece-of-crap-poor-excuse-of-a-human-being... I'm not here to play games with you. I want to know where Vickie is, and if you don't tell me..."

"You'll what?" Phil interrupted. "You'll beat me to a pulp?... Ooooh, I'm so scared." He laughed.

Sal, with his hands still on his shirt pushed him against the wall. "I know I've been a passive idiot in your eyes, but I'm here to tell you that I mean business. I'm not playing games and if beating you to a pulp is what I have to do, then I will." Sal stared him down.

"First of all, get your hands off me," Phil said as he pushed Sal away. "You have no idea who you're messing with."

"Are you going to kill me, Phil? Because that would be quicker than the slow death I've suffered during my entire relationship with Vickie."

"I told you the truth; she's not here."

"Where is she then?"

"I'm not sure. We got into a fight, and she stormed out. You know how she gets."

Sal fought the urge to slug him. "What happened?"

Phil walked over to the couch again and sat back down. "I told her what I did with Rose, she got jealous, and stormed out. I mean, I did it for her."

"You manipulated Rose and slept with her for Vickie? You're a piece of work. You slept with her to get back at me because you're a..."

"Hey, watch it. I did what I did because she was jealous of her. She hated the fact that you wouldn't give up the relationship for her. Don't blame me if you made your wife suspicious."

"That's rich considering her *relationship* with you. She's my wife, and I don't need to justify anything to you." Sal walked towards the door. "I'll be back."

"Make sure when you do you come prepared."

Sal turned around and came back into the apartment. "You're threatening me?"

"I don't make threats, Boys Scout. What I do is take care of what is mine at all costs. Can you say the same?"

"If anything happens to her..."

"You're funny. You bust in here blowing smoke up my butt with your empty threats. You think I'm afraid of you?" Phil stood up, walked over to Sal. "You should be afraid of me. You've already seen what I'm capable of."

Sal turned to leave, but suddenly turned back and punched Phil in the face so hard that Phil lost his footing and landed on the floor.

The surprised look on Phil's face said it all. "No! You don't know what I'm capable of when it comes to protecting my family," Sal replied.

Vickie was on the floor in the corner of a dark, musky room. She heard voices, but wasn't sure what was being said. Vickie's breathing labored. Sweat ran down her face. "It's so cold in here." She heard herself say.

"It's okay, baby. You're okay."

"Who's there?"

"It's Juicy."

Vickie laughed. "What kind of name is Juicy?"

"Hey, you didn't seem to mind my name when you were using my heroin."

"It's cold, Juicy." She shivered. "Why is it so cold?" Suddenly she threw up violently all over Juicy's shoes.

"Ah, man. You've made a mess... Crap! Porter is going to go ballistic, man. You gotta go."

"Go... go where?"

"I don't care." He grabbed her by her arm and dragged her out of the apartment. "Go back to Phil and let him clean up your mess." He slammed the door in her face.

"Hey, open up!" Vickie yelled as she pounded on the door. She was not well. She tried to make it down the hall to Phil's, but she passed out in the hall.

Sal heard Vickie's voice and ran down the hall toward her voice. When he got there, she was passed out on the floor. He could smell the stench of vomit and knew she had overdone it. He knelt down and took her pulse. It was slow. He tried to wake her, but she didn't move. He panicked and picked her up and rushed towards the elevator. "Hang in there, Vickie. I swear it's going to be all right."

Chapter 28

Sal couldn't help but pace outside the emergency room doors. On the drive to the hospital, all he could do was pray that Vickie would wake up, but nothing happened. He found himself in yet another situation where he was worried for her life. Afterwards, he would promise himself that he would leave her, but never found the strength to do so. He couldn't get away from the promises he had made on his wedding day—'til death do us part. He was the man. He was the hero. He had to try until his last breath to love her, to cross the river, to slay the dragon, and to climb the tower. One thing his father taught him was that a good man always kept his promises. The doctor came over to him.

"How is she?" Sal pleaded.

"Mr. Martinelli, she's not out of the woods yet. We've treated her with Naloxone."

His heart skipped a beat.

"Mr. Martinelli, did you hear me?"

"Yes... what's that you gave her?"

"It's a drug we use to combat drug overdoses, but she's still non-responsive."

"Is there anything else you can do?"

"We're doing everything we can for her. We'll be admitting her as soon as a room is available."

"When can I see her?"

"After she's admitted. Rest assured, we're doing everything we can."

"Thank you, doctor. I'm sure you are."

No matter how many times he'd been through this, it continued to be the hardest thing he had ever faced. The room started to spin, and he felt the floor on his backside.

"Are you okay? Let's get a chair for this man." He heard the doctor's voice through his haze.

"No... no, I'm fine, really." There were too many people that surrounded him. It felt as if the walls had closed in around him. Sal just wanted some air. He walked briskly out through the emergency room doors. The fresh air slapped him on the face. It shook him up from the slumber his mind was in. He walked over to a bench and plopped down.

"Hello." Came a calming, familiar voice. Sal looked up to find Henry.

"How did you know I... never mind, of course you knew."

"How is she?"

"I'm not sure. The doctor said she's nonresponsive, whatever that means... you wouldn't be able to tell me if she's going to make it or not?"

"Sal, I'm here for you. Her life... your life... my life... it's in His hands, not mine. I'm not a fortuneteller. I only know what He wants me to know."

"I know. I know. I don't know if I have it in me to believe. I'm... I'm... just lost..."

"If you don't mind an old man's company, I'd like to stay here with you. We don't have to talk."

Sal couldn't explain it, but this man seemed to emanate peace. He felt better, stronger, as he sat next to him. He felt safe. He decided that he needed to talk, and so he did. He filled Henry in on all that had transpired with Phil, Rose, Joey, and Vickie. The more he spoke, the lighter he felt.

"Thank you, Henry, for listening. Sometimes it helps to have Jesus with skin on... not that you're Jesus, but you know... I mean a person..."

"I understand what you mean."

"You've helped me see a side of God I hadn't known before—the supernatural side. If He could tell you to come here just for me, then He must really love me."

"Of course He does, Sal. You can't make choices for Vickie, but you can be there for her... if she lets you."

"I'll fight for her with all that's within me."

"Good, I'm glad to hear that. I'm heading back home, but if you ever need me... well, let's just say I'll be in touch." He smiled a crooked smile that made Sal chuckle.

He watched as Henry walked away. He appreciated how he listened, and showed compassion without a preachy attitude. He wanted to be a better man after he talked to Henry. He was the first person he had met that reminded him of the Jesus he had read about in the Bible.

"Hey, Sal." He turned his head and saw Rose. His heart sank. Sal's guilt about Phil consumed him. "How's Vickie?" she asked with genuine concern in her voice.

"I was going to go inside to see if there is any change in her condition. How are you doing?"

"I made my own choices, and now I'm faced with the consequences." She swallowed hard and took a deep breath. "I don't consider this child a curse or punishment. From this day forward I'm taking one step at a time, and I will make the best possible life for my child that I can. I'm already in love with him or her."

"You're remarkable."

"I don't feel remarkable." She sighed. "Let's go see how your wife is doing."

Sal walked inside with Rose. Vickie's bed was empty. *How long was I outside for?* He ran out to the nurse's station. "Excuse me, nurse. Where's my wife, Vickie Martinelli? She's not in the room."

She looked up the name on her computer. "She's been moved upstairs to Room 614."

Sal was horrified that for a split second he felt both relieved and terrified at the same time. He didn't know that was possible. "Is she okay?"

"I'm sorry sir, it doesn't say, just that she's been moved. You can take the elevator located down the corridor to your left."

Sal ran for the elevator. Rose followed. "Look Sal, if she's awake, I'm the last person she would want to see. I'm going home. Let me know if I can do anything."

"Okay." The elevator doors opened. "Rose." She turned around. "Thank you for your friendship."

"I'm leaving town," she blurted out.

Sal held the door so it wouldn't close. "What? Why?"

"I need a fresh start and it would be best for this baby if Phil never found out I was pregnant. It's best for everybody."

Sal didn't know what to say. He selfishly wanted her to stay, but understood why she would leave. "I pray everything works out for you, Rose."

"Thanks, Sal. I hope it works out for you too."

"Don't be a stranger," she said softly. He knew that he probably wouldn't see her again.

The last thing Sal saw was Rose's smile as the elevator doors closed. It felt like an eternity to reach the sixth floor. As soon as the doors opened, Sal read the signs on the wall to see which direction Room 614 was. He walked briskly, and as he approached her room, his heart sank in his chest. He couldn't breathe. Vickie's eyes were opened. She looked at him, then immediately turned her head to stare out the window. He walked slowly to her bedside. He placed his hand on hers. She didn't move it away, but didn't look at him either. "I love you, Vickie." A tear ran down her face. "I love you with all that's within me."

She looked at him. For the first time Sal saw brokenness in her eyes. "For the life of me, I don't understand why? I tricked you into marrying me, passed off another man's child as yours... I've betrayed you with other men... and the cherry on top is I'm a drug addict. So, why would you love me?"

"To be honest, I sometimes don't understand myself." This made Vickie laugh. "I know that my faith has made my love for you stronger. I took the vows we made to each other very seriously. No matter what a DNA test may prove, Joey is my son, and he always will be. I'm his father... period, end of story."

"I know I need help. I don't want to disappoint you and Joey again."

"You have to do this for you—Vickie. You need to be healthy for your sake. Your body almost didn't recover this time."

"You're right, but I don't deserve any more chances, Sal."

"Vickie... look at me." She gazed into his eyes. He wanted to make sure she heard him. "If you had cancer, I would love you and be by your side as you received chemo. This isn't any different. We're dealing with an illness, and I'm here to help you get better. No more back and forth or ultimatums. I'm here... period."

Sal wasn't sure what would happen next or whether his marriage would survive. He knew that he needed to try to be strong for all their sakes. She held his hand, and his heart leaped into his throat.

"I've been horrible to you. I've placed Joey in danger by my actions... I've been... no, I am selfish. I was alone and on my own for a long time... that doesn't matter... it's just excuses." Tears ran down her face. She held Sal's hand tightly. "I've said sorry hundreds of times, but I've never really meant it... not once. So what would be the use now? I need to show you and Joey that I want to change. I'm ready to do that now... finally. This time, it scared me... the lack of control... it has to stop. I do love you, Sal." For the first time since they had met, those words sounded sincere.

He got choked up, but managed to respond with, "I love you, too." *Did she really just say that? Was his mind playing tricks on him?* He thanked God silently in his heart for the miracle he had just witnessed.

Nadine Zawacki

Epilogue

Sal could hear the raindrops as they fell on the awning outside the candy store. He sat on a stool behind the counter where Margaret had sat for more years than he could count. It had been two years since she passed away, and he still couldn't find anyone quite like her to work at the store. He tried, but no one worked out. He looked up when he heard the door chime. It was as if time froze. It had been ten years, but time had been good to Rose. She looked the same except for the noticeable bump in her belly. Beside her stood a little girl wearing a raincoat with a hood. She pulled her hood down, and there stood a miniature Rose. Her auburn hair was tied up in a ponytail. Her blue eyes sparkled like her mother's.

"Mommy, can I pick out any candy that I want?" she asked with excitement.

"Yes, honey you can. Maybe you can pick out something to bring to grandma's house."

"Yeah!"

Sal was speechless. The last time he had seen Rose was that day in the hospital. She approached the counter. "Hi, Sal."

"Rose... it's good to see you. You look great!"

"Thanks," she smiled. "So do you."

"She looks just like you." He looked in the little girl's direction. "What's her name?"

"I named her Hope."

"That's a pretty name. So have you moved back?"

"No, just visiting my mom. She's thinking of moving back with us to Chicago."

"Wow. That would be a big change for her."

"Yeah, she's a New Yorker through and through, but wants to be closer to her grandchildren."

"Grandchildren?"

"Yeah. I'm pregnant. I'm married to a wonderful man. We met after I moved. He was so patient with me about all that I had gone through. He was even there when I gave birth. He's loved Hope as if she were his own."

"Sounds like you found a good one," he said. After an awkward pause Sal asked, "How's your sister?"

"She's married and is the mother of twin boys, believe it or not. Her husband is a lieutenant in the army. They live in Hawaii."

"I'm sure that's a hardship for her." He chuckled. "You seem so peaceful and... happy."

"I am," she smiled. "How about you and Vickie?" Sal's expression changed. "I'm sorry. Loaded question."

"No. It's okay. She died three years ago."

"Oh, Sal, I'm so sorry. I didn't know."

"After she got out of the hospital, she went to rehab. It was a miracle. She did so well. We had another child, a boy. Joey just loves him to pieces. He's very protective of his little brother." Sal's mind wandered. He was lost in thought. Rose's voice bought him back to the present.

"Sal, are you okay?"

"I'm fine. She um... loved me in the end. She was so healthy. Our family was healed, then one day... a brain aneurysm... one moment she was here... then the next she was gone."

"I'm so sorry for your loss."

"I'm doing better now. I met this lovely woman in church last year. She loves the kids. She has two boys. Her husband died and... anyway, I'm planning on asking her to marry me."

"Well, then I guess congratulations are in order. That's wonderful news."

"Thanks, it is. I think she'll say 'yes'." A smile came back across his face. "I don't know if you heard, but Phil was killed about eight years ago during a drug deal gone bad... at least that's what the police believe."

"No, I didn't know that. I can't say that I'm surprised."

"Mommy, I picked out chocolate for me and for grandma."

"Good choices." She smiled at Hope, and continued, "This is an old friend of mine, Mr. Martinelli."

"Nice to meet you Mr. Martinelli. Is this your store?"

"It's nice to meet you too. Yes, this is my store."

"You have the best store in the whole world!" Hope said with excitement.

Sal found her to be as charming as her mother. "Why, thank you."

"How much do I owe you?"

"Sorry, Rose, you're money isn't good here."

"Sal, please..." He shook his head. "Thank you."

As she turned to leave a very handsome young man came in through the door with a little boy that looked like Sal. They were both wet from the rain.

"Hey, Pops," Joey said.

"Hey, Pops." The little boy imitated his older brother.

"Hey, guys. You look a bit wet. What happened to your raincoat and umbrella?"

"The umbrella broke, and David here couldn't find his raincoat. Apparently there is a black hole in the back of the closet in his classroom."

"I gave it to Betty. She didn't have a raincoat, and I didn't want my girlfriend to get wet."

Joey rolled his eyes. "That's dumb."

"Joseph, don't call your brother dumb. He was being gallant."

"What's that mean, Daddy?"

"It means you were being a little gentleman by being kind to a lady." David stuck his tongue out at Joey. "Settle down, you two. I want you to..." Sal was about to introduce them to Rose, but she had left.

"You want what?" Joey asked.

"Never mind. Okay, you two, let's get you home and out of those wet clothes. I'll close up early today."

Acknowledgements

I want to thank all my friends who read the rough drafts of this book for their positive feedback, especially Candice Fowler, Erica Berthen, Teressa Peters and Tom Zawacki.

Thank you Tom Schultz for all the work you put into helping me get this book in print. Without your connections and support this book would not have happened. I appreciate both your time and generous support. Thank you Jill Schultz, who helped with final proofreading. You both have been such a delight to me.

Thank you, Dianna Clark, for the photo on the back cover.

I want to thank my children Lisa and Tom Zawacki for their love, support and belief in me.

I want to thank my husband Tom, whose love and encouragement make it possible to write stories. Your support has helped bring this book to completion.

Finally, I want to thank God for creativity and inspiration to write.

CPSIA information can be obtained at www.ICGtesting.com
Printed in the USA
LVOW04s0730200115

423566LV00005B/35/P

9 781987 852004